# Enchanted Gift

# Enchanted Gift

## *The Secret of the Castle*

Merita Dragusha

iUniverse, Inc.
Bloomington

**Enchanted Gift**
The Secret of the Castle

iUniverse books may be ordered through booksellers or by contacting:

iUniverse
1663 Liberty Drive
Bloomington, IN 47403
www.iuniverse.com
1-800-Authors (1-800-288-4677)

ISBN: 978-1-4401-9535-8 (sc)
ISBN: 978-1-4401-9537-2 (hc)
ISBN: 978-1-4401-9536-5 (ebk)

Printed in the United States of America

iUniverse rev. date: 01/04/2013

# CONTENTS

CHAPTER 1 ....................................................................................1

CHAPTER 2 ....................................................................................5

CHAPTER 3 ....................................................................................14

CHAPTER 4 ....................................................................................21

CHAPTER 5 ....................................................................................30

CHAPTER 6 ....................................................................................37

CHAPTER 7 ....................................................................................42

CHAPTER 8 ....................................................................................49

CHAPTER 9 ....................................................................................54

CHAPTER 10 ..................................................................................70

# CHAPTER 1

There was an old wooden hut that could be found on the flat top of a hill in the village that was called Bedolia. A couple (Sorne and Zara) lived inside who loved each other dearly, and desperately wanted children. Every day they walked down the hill to the market, just to see the other people's children. Sometimes they loved to play with them, but they wished to have their own child. They kept wishing for twenty years.

One morning a woman with a small brown bag knocked on their door. Although she was a stranger, they welcomed her into their hut. The strange woman was wearing a long gray dress and had a scarf tied around her head. She had a sad look on her face. It seemed that she was worried about something. She stayed silent as she went to sit at the table on a little wooden stool, and then she said with trembling lips, "I know you have been wishing for something for a long time, and I brought a gift for you that can make your wish come true."

Sorne and Zara didn't say anything. They just looked at each other with uneasy faces.

"Do you want to wish for something?" the woman asked Zara.

Zara started to walk toward the window. She could not think of anything at that moment, but after a short bit of silence, she turned and met Sorne's eyes. She remembered her wish.

"I want to know. Where did you get that gift that you want to give to us?" Sorne asked the woman before Zara spoke.

"A woman came to my house like I came to yours now," said the strange woman as she was looking down at the bag. "She told me everything she knew about this gift, and told me to make a wish. I felt weird at first when

1

I saw it, but I accepted it anyway. A few days later, I began to see many surprises every day and finally my wish came true."

Zara moved quickly in circles around the room as she was staring at the bag. From the time that the strange woman came into her house, she had feelings in her heart. She was jumping at the chance to make her wish.

Sorne could not believe what the strange woman was saying, but before he asked her to leave his house, he asked, "Since your wish came true, why do you want to give away that special thing that you are talking about? I don't understand you at all. If I believed in the gift, I would not give it away."

"I cannot keep it anymore. I have to give it to someone so they can be happy too," said the woman.

Zara jumped in, "Show us the gift, I want to see it."

The strange woman, not waiting to be asked twice, quickly opened the bag and took out the gift. "This is a flower. You may make your wish now," she said as she looked at Zara.

Sorne started to laugh and said, "This is a flower? I don't believe it. You are calling this a gift?"

The woman became very sad when she saw Sorne was laughing. The gift that she wanted to give to them, it didn't look like anything special or something amazing. It was just a stick as thin as a pencil about eight inches long resting in the cup.

She took a deep breath and said, "It will improve later on, and you will be surprised with it." She tried very hard to make them take the flower.

Zara believed everything the strange woman said. As soon as the strange woman had opened the bag Zara had already made her wish. She could not let go of that special gift which she was so happy to hear about.

It was hard for Sorne and Zara to believe in something that was impossible, but after they accepted the gift, a few days later, it started to change their lives. Zara become pregnant, just as they had hoped.

The unbelievable gift did make their wish of many years come true.

After nine months, Sorne and Zara had a baby boy in their house, and they named him Lanti. He was the best thing that had ever happened to them. He was a beautiful child. Everybody loved him, especially his mom and dad. Every time Sorne walked down the hill to the market with Lanti, the people stopped to look at Lanti and were very happy to see him, but they were also very concerned about the strange light was shining from the inside of that family's hut at night. Even though they were curious, no one was willing to go near the house to find out what was going on.

Zara never left her house alone since her wish had come true. She stayed inside and cooked good meals for Sorne and Lanti every day.

Lanti grew up and was now 11 years old. He spent most of his time working and playing at the market and he really worked hard to help his dad make a living. He was too young to work much, but the important thing was that he had lots of fun. He never really felt ill, at least not until one day Zara decided to go to the market with him and Sorne.

A woman who lived at the bottom of the hill in the small house was looking out her window. She saw them leave and decided she would go into their hut to find out where the light was coming from. She waited until they were out of sight before heading up to their hut. When she reached the hut she stood at the door but got a feeling that she should not go inside. She quickly opened the door and went inside even though she wanted to turn back.

As soon as she entered she saw a wondrous sight. She started rubbing her eyes and after a minute left the hut and fell to the ground. She became scared when she realized that she couldn't see anything around her. She started to scream as she realized that she was now blind.

After a short time Sorne and Zara returned with Lanti. Sorne was walking very fast caring Lanti in his arms and Zara was following them. Lanti was not feeling good. He was having trouble moving his arms and legs, and his face was burning up.

Before they reached their hut, Zara heard something moving behind the bushes. She stopped and looked. She saw the woman sitting on the ground, crying and wiping her face and she was burning up. Immediately Zara asked her, "What is wrong with you lady?" The woman did not know it was Zara because she couldn't see her, but she told her the truth. She had been in Zara's house saw something that made her blind and ill. When Zara heard her words, she almost fell on the ground from fear. Immediately she grabbed the woman's arm and said, "Come with me into my house, I will help you," and took her into her house. A minute later Zara came out of her house holding the brown bag in her hand. She started walking down the hill as fast as she could, not looking back. Zara had to do exactly as the strange woman told her to do, because it was time for Zara to pass the gift to someone else.

# CHAPTER 2

## Three months earlier

The city of Vollgory was located nine kilometers from the village of Bedolia. It had a huge castle with high walls made of strong stones located on the flat top of the hill. It was surrounded by a moat with the only entrance being a drawbridge with a big turret on the top.

Inside lived the King and his name was Vollg. He was known to be very sincere and extremely kind. He stood six feet tall with blue eyes and a long white beard. He was not handsome but had a pleasant face. He was married to queen Solia and they had a daughter by the name of Artella.

Early one morning in the imperial room, the king was sitting at the table, which was only three yards from the windows. He was staring at swords that were hanging on the right side of the wall, and thinking about something that he had kept secret for a long time. Suddenly he stood up and moved to open the door.

Outside the door, an armed guard stood. He was wearing a tailored uniform and had a sword strapped to his left hip. His name was Sandri. He was only eighteen years old. He had dark brown hair with almond-shaped brown eyes, and was as tall as the king. He only had a few months of experience working at the castle. Usually he stood guard outside, but today he was commanded to stay inside the castle by the imperial door. As he was walking left and right, suddenly he heard a soft voice from the door behind him. "I need you to go and retrieve my daughter immediately." When Sandri turned to see who was speaking, he almost fainted when he saw the king standing in front of him. It was the first time that he had met the king face to face. He quickly came to attention and dropped to one knee saying, "Yes my lord, I will go immediately," and left to fetch the princess.

Upon reaching the princess's room, he slowly opened the door without announcing his presence. He approached the princess's bed. He could see that the windows were open and a zephyr was blowing on her face. He stopped next to her bed and looked at her beautiful face. Her beauty dazzled him. He thought to himself that he would like to be the wind and caress her beautiful hair. At that moment, the princess woke up and found the guard looking at her. She screamed in fear and rose quickly from the bed and said, "Why are you in my room? What do you want here?" and she pulled the blanket quickly all the way up to her mouth.

Sandri moved back a step. His eyes grew wide and his heart began to race when he saw her awake.

Quickly he came to attention and dropped to one knee, and said, "Your majesty, please forgive my intrusion but the king wants to speak with you immediately."

The princess frowned at him and stated, "You will never enter my room without knocking. If you knock and I give you permission to enter then you may do so but otherwise do not darken my door. Now you may go and I will prepare myself to see the king. Do not ever enter without permission again."

"Yes, your majesty," Sandri said as he walked out of the room and closed the door behind him.

The Princess rose from her bed. She loved beautiful things, so dressed herself beautifully every day in a costly manner. Today she chose a brocaded sky-blue dress that fit her perfectly. She was five feet tall with a beautifully sculptured face and almond-shaped blue eyes and coal black hair that hung down her back.

As she left her room the princess noticed that the guard was still by the door waiting for her. In a scared voice, she asked, "Why are you here waiting for me?"

Sandri responded, "Because, I was sent by the king, I need to escort you back to the king your majesty."

The princess laughed and said, "I know the way to my father's room. I live here. Do you think that I cannot find my way there?"

Sandri did not respond but just walked behind her throughout the castle.

The king waited patiently in the imperial room for his daughter to appear. Finally the princess entered the room with Sandri walking behind her.

The king rose as a way to honor her. "Come sit near me my daughter, I need to talk to you about something," he said.

The princess bowed her head and went to sit on the chair close to her father. After she sat down, she looked at Sandri and smiled at him. She realized that he was a new guard and he still did not understand his job.

Sandri's job was to stand outside the door and not inside the imperial room, but he could not seem to pull himself away from the princess. He stood close to her, smiling and looking into her beautiful blue eyes. In his fascination, he had even forgotten that the king was in the room.

Before the king went to sit on his chair, he saw Sandri was still staring at his daughter. Slowly he went over to Sandri, tapped him on the shoulder and laughed as he said, "You can go now, and do not forget to close the door fully behind you."

"Yes, My lord," Sandri answered as he bowed his head and began to walk toward the door while still watching the princess out of the corner of his eye. Then he closed the door slowly behind him.

The king started his talk. "Listen very well my daughter. My father had been an extremely smart and powerful king. He had been at war for several years but finally defeated his enemies. Then he had this castle built. Before he died, he shared the secret of the castle and taught me the rules of being a king. So under the castle are three rooms that no one knows about."

The princess stood silent until her father stopped talking, and then quietly asked him, "Why do you want to tell me this secret now, father?"

"I have been waiting for just the right moment to tell you, and today you are the same age as I was when my father told me forty years ago," the king replied.

"How can it be possible that you told no one about this for all these years?" asked the princess.

"I keep my promises," responded the king. "I promised my father that I would never share this secret with anyone except my child when they turned sixteen, so today is the day for you to see it."

The princess was so excited that she could barely stand still and hurried her father along the corridor of the castle. As they arrived near her room, the princess looked at her father with a shocked expression on her face. She thought that the secret was in her room and told him that goose bumps had covered her body at the thought of the secret being in her room.

The king laughed and stated, "No, we have a bit farther to go my daughter, don't worry, you will see everything."

As they walked along the long wall with the red tiles, they came upon two swords that were hanging on the wall. One was located on the right side of the wall and the other on left with a gas lamp set between them.

"You may have seen those swords many times before, but you didn't know what they were there for. Now I will tell you of their importance and how you can use them," said the king as he removed the right sword from its place. "This sword is the key that opens the door. It is one door that you may not recognize at all." He pushed the wall just an inch and stepped aside to show that the wall was actually a door.

The princess was surprised. She had always wondered why those two swords were hanging on the wall, but never thought that there would be a door behind them.

The king took the sword and lamp then they entered in. It was dark inside, but the lamp had enough light to see everything.

Slowly the king closed the door behind him, and locked it with the sword that he had in his hand. He turned and looked at the princess saying, "Do not worry, if someone tries to push this wall, the door will not open in any way, because the sword is the key on both sides of the door."

The princess didn't say anything. She just shook her head and remained silent.

Inside were some stairs built from stones with steps wide enough for three people to walk on them at the same time. Ahead there were three small rooms without doors. The first two rooms were four meters long by four meters wide and empty without even a window.

When they entered the last room, it was only slightly larger than the first and second room. The only thing the princess could see was a wooden box lying on the floor near a corner and a small door to the left.

The king took two steps to the right. He pulled an iron handle from the rope that was hung in the corner, and opened three small windows at the same time. Through them immediately came fresh air and the room started to seem better even with the light.

"It is nice father, I can see much better now," said the princess.

The king sat on the floor near the wooden box. He slowly opened it. Inside were many beautiful things of gold and silver that belonged to the king.

He picked up a necklace with a big shiny white diamond, and raised it in front of his daughter to show it to her.

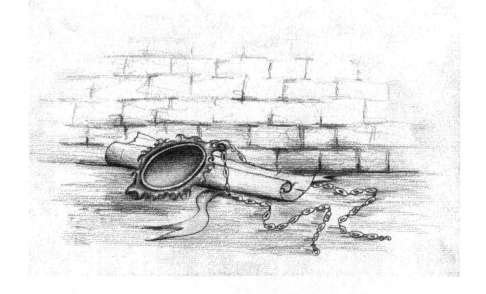

The princess looked surprised. "It looks very beautiful," she said as she raised her hand to touch it. "Who has worn this before?" she asked her father.

"My mother was the queen of our country, a strong and powerful woman. She wore this necklace all the time, just like I wear my crown. I asked her many times why she wore this every day and she told me this was her lucky necklace," said the king as he raised the necklace near the princess, and put it on her neck. "And now, this is yours. You are the luckiest girl in the world."

The princess was very happy. She turned, and embraced her father. With a full smile on her face she said, "I will never take this necklace from my neck father. I'm very happy and lucky that you are my father."

"It is time to leave my daughter, but before we go, I want to also tell you this," the king said as he rose up, and moved to the small door on the left.

"On the other side of this door, is a tunnel that can lead you out of the castle."

"I have only been in there once, but if we go through this tunnel, we will see mountains. We don't have time to go today, because it is a very long road."

"Yes father, another day, so we will now go upstairs," said the princess with a happy face. She could not wait to get out of there, so she could see the necklace better.

As they emerged from secret place and closed the door behind them, the king turned to face the princess and spoke in a low voice, "Listen, you cannot go inside any time you want, this is only if there is any danger, and you cannot tell your mother of this. If she knew, she would get upset, because, I kept the secret from her for so long."

The princess bowed her head saying, "I promise father that I will not tell anyone of this. I will keep it in my heart and never forget it."

They left each other. The princess went to her room and the king began to walk toward the imperial room.

Recently the king had been having days when he did not feel well. On those days something tightened in his chest, but he did not tell anybody. He did not want anybody to worry about him.

When the king got to the imperial room, he saw the queen was sitting in her chair waiting for him. She stood up and said, "I was looking for you, but couldn't find you anywhere."

"Why do you need to see me?" asked the king.

"I just wanted to know where you were when you did not come to eat breakfast with me," she said.

The king was silent as he walked slowly across the room toward the window, touching his chest that was bothering him.

The queen saw him struggling something awful, so she went near him and said, "Are you all right?"

"Yes. I am all right. Just a little bit tired," said the king.

"Do you want some water?" she asked.

He didn't answer.

"I am going to the kitchen to get some water," the queen said as she helped him sit on a chair and very quickly left the room. As she was walking in the hallway, she cast her eyes toward the windows. A beam came directly into her eyes. She stopped and approached the window.

Outside it was a very beautiful day. The princess had just gone out for a walk in the courtyard of the castle. The sunlight was falling on the princess's necklace and distributing rays on all sides, so the ray that the queen saw was coming from her daughter's neck.

The queen said to herself while watching her daughter from the window, "I told her not to touch my necklace, but she still did not listen to me." She got angry.

The princess noticed that her mother was watching her through the window, so she thought she better go back inside and see why her mother kept watching her.

The queen left the window. Before she reached the kitchen, she saw her daughter coming inside. She stopped and waited to meet her.

After they met each other, the queen saw that her daughter did not have her necklace. Immediately she asked her, "Tell me, who gave you this necklace that you are wearing?"

The princess answered with a soft smiling voice, "Father gave it to me. See how beautiful it is!" The queen was very surprised because she had never seen this necklace full of diamonds before. She went near, and looked at it. "It is very beautiful, but to my knowledge you cannot wear the necklace before you are married," she said to her daughter.

The princess put her head down, and raised her hand to hold up her necklace "Yes mother but father wanted me to keep it. It was his mother's and he liked me to have it as a present from him," the princess answered. She saw her mother became jealous, and she did not talk to her anymore but started going in the direction of her room.

The queen returned to the room where the king was. She looked confused and stood near as she was, wrinkling in her forehead. She asked, "Where exactly did you have that necklace that our daughter has put on her neck?"

The King smiled at her and said, "That necklace was my mother's. You know my mother wanted us to have a girl, but she died before she was born."

The queen was walking toward the window and saying, "I've never seen it before, why did you keep it secret?"

"Before my mother died, she took my hand and put the necklace in it and she said to me, if you have a girl, please, when she grows up give this to her. I promised my mother that I would save it until I had a daughter. So my daughter is grown up now and I gave it to her," said the king as he was looking at her, "Did you bring me some water or not? I thought you went for some."

"Yes, I'm going now," she said.

The king could never tell her of the secret he had, because sometime she raised her voice against him. Maybe she was a good person, but the king never trusted her.

After a week, hard pain tortured the king. He had a disease that made him silent and immovable. He was lying in bed, covered with a white cover, and remained very ill without any power to open his eyes. He looked like he was at death's door.

Everyone was worried about him, but mostly the princess. She stayed in his room day and night by his side. Sometimes she talked to him even though he could not answer or look at her. She told him of her feelings and that she had always loved him.

The king was taking his last breaths, as he was near the end of his life. He stayed in his bed for three days and three nights without moving. On the last night the king opened his eyes time after time, trying to breathe through his mouth as he stared at the princess without talking.

The princess was happy when she saw him open his eyes, but she did not understand that he already had stretched out his hands and was knocking at death's door.

"Father I know that you will wake up," she said. But in vain, he looked at her once and turned his eyes to the ceiling of the room and froze in the moment.

His heart wasn't beating. He wasn't breathing anymore. His soul had left him.

The princess began to cry with all her strength. "Lord, please help my father," she prayed. "I don't want him to die." She squeezed her eyes shut and pressed her face to his chest for a moment, then kissed him twice on his forehead. Her tears, which she could not hold back, fell like rain on his body.

Two soldiers were outside the room standing in front of the door. They heard a sad noise, and rushed into the room and pulled the princess from the king. At that moment, the queen came into the room. She went to her daughter, who was weeping and lying on the floor from the pain of her father's death. She took her in her arms and embraced her as a child, saying, "Do not cry my child, there is nothing you can do other than accept this." Immediately the queen told her soldiers, "Please take Artella to her room and take care of her until she recovers."

After the soldiers left the room with the princess, the queen remained in the room with the dead body of the king. She started to cry as well, laying her head on his chest and thinking of him. Early the next morning, the front yard of the castle was crowded with old and young people who loved the king. The news of the death of the king spread very quickly in the city and surrounding villages.

When the queen came out, all the people remained quiet. They were trying to listen to what the queen was going to say.

As the queen was getting ready to speak, first she squeezed her eyes shut for a moment and then opened them. She was trying to keep herself strong in front of the people, and not faint in front of them. "Today is a sad day for all of us," she said as she looked at the people. "I am glad to see so many of you here. Last night our beloved king's duties ended, and now I will assume the duties of governing our country. I will try to be as the king was. He has been a very stout man, with strong, noble behavior. He always knew that all of you loved him very much." Then there was a break in her voice. Her whole body started trembling. Two soldiers were standing near her. They saw that she could not stand anymore, so they grabbed her by the arms gently, and they walked her inside the castle. A little later in the day, soldiers burned the body of the king. It was the end of the king.

# CHAPTER 3

A month after the king's death, the princess decided to go for a walk. She loved to walk through the yard and enjoy her day, but she was still sad about her father.

As she was walking, she saw the guard Sandri standing at the front of the imperial doors. She remembered that particular moment when he had entered her room without knocking and had frightened her. In that moment immediately she started to smile. She approached him slowly, smiling at him. "I'm so happy to see you again," she said to him.

Sandri began to tremble when he saw her standing in front of him. Quickly he knelt down on his knees, bowed his head, and said, "Good afternoon, your majesty."

"Good afternoon," she said as she looked down at him, and noticed how nervous he was. She started to laugh, "Don't worry, I just want to see you." She tried to calm him down, "You do not need to kneel before me, and you can call me Artella, if you want to."

Sandri was surprised by her. He bowed again. He forgot what she said. "Yes Artella," he replied.

"May I please know your name?" she asked him.

He looked at her, and after a bit of silence, he gently and calmly said, "I have the name of my father. He died before I was born. My mother was happy and sad at the same time when I was born, because she had nothing to give me from my father. The only thing he had left her was his name. So now I live with my father's name, Sandri."

"You have a beautiful name," said the princess as she looked at him. "Does your mother remember your father every time she calls your name?

"Yes, she did, but not anymore. She died a few years ago," Sandri answered.

"Remember, life goes on even without your parents. Look at me. I'm still sad about my father, but I have to come out and talk to other people to feel better," said the princess without breaking her voice. She started to feel much stronger than she had been as she started talking with Sandri.

She realized that she was not the only one who had lost a father.

Hours went by while Sandri and the princess were together. They walked around the castle yard talking about all the things that had happened to them while growing up. This was an amazing day for them. The days became more and more special for the princess since she started hanging out with Sandri. She loved talking with him, and the time she spent with him was the best time she had ever had.

From the first day that they had begun talking, a love was born between them. But neither one was willing to explain it to the other, at least not until one afternoon. The princess was in her room with a servant, changing her dress. She heard a knock at the door. When she opened it she saw Sandri. Her whole body began trembling from seeing him. She could not speak a word. After a few seconds of silence she said, "Yes, come in please."

Sandri smiled and greeted her as he walked into the room. He jumped and stopped where he was. "Well," he said, as he rubbed his hair. "When I thought about coming to your room I didn't consider that you might not be alone." And then he looked at the servant. The servant smiled and asked him, "What do you want here?"

Before Sandri said anything the princess quickly went over to the servant and with a lowered voice said to her, "You can go now."

The servant without a word bowed her head and left the room, closing the door behind her.

In the room, there remained only the princess and Sandri. There was a silence as they just looked at each other. Slowly the princess approached him, and looked at him with beautiful lucid blue eyes. They began with brief kisses, and then much longer ones. All of a sudden, they broke off the kissing, because they knew that they were making a big mistake. They could not love each other, or marry without the queen's approval. The princess was not allowed to marry a guard, or anyone who was not a member of the Royal Family. The man she had begun to fall in love with was not suitable to marry her since he was only a guard. However, the princess began secretly being with Sandri. They met each other in a corner of the castle every day, somewhere that no one would see or hear them. They thought that no one could know, but after two weeks, seeing them together, the queen started to become suspicious. She tried to find a way to separate them before it was too late.

She went outside of the imperial doors where Sandri was standing. With a lower voice she said to him, "I want to talk to you privately, please."

"Yes, my lady," Sandri answered. He followed her until they had stepped into the imperial room. The queen wanted to speak, but before she did, she turned and closed the door behind her. "I don't completely understand what's going on with you and my daughter. I want to know the truth."

Sandri was standing near the corner of the imperial table. His thoughts circulated inside his head but he wasn't able to tell her the truth. He was shaking like a child out of fear.

"Please, my lady," said Sandri as he looked at her. "Believe me, there is nothing between me and Artella."

"I don't believe you at all," said the queen as she was looking at him with an angry face. "I have seen you with her from the first day. I was happy at first to see my daughter talking to someone, but seeing you together every day is not what I had hoped for."

"My lady," said Sandri before he noticed the queen raising her hand in front of him.

"I don't want you to talk anymore," said the queen, as she went to sit on her chair. "Let me tell you something."

Sandri stood frozen in place, looking at the queen. He was in a difficult position.

"My daughter is a young girl. She is learning. Someday she will be a queen and I do not want her to make a mistake," said the queen as she looked at him.

"You understand that you two are as different as night and day. I command you to leave the castle as soon as possible!"

Sandri's face began to change color. He wanted to say something but changed his mind. He just asked her, "Could I please have one more chance my lady and I will fix this?"

"No, today is the day that you are going to finish your military term," said the queen, moving her head slowly from side to side. "I want you to leave tomorrow and do not say anything to my daughter about this."

"Yes, my lady," said Sandri as he rubbed the sweat from his forehead and bowed his head. He could not say anything more. He had to follow her ruling.

Sandri left the room and shut the door behind him. He could not believe what had just happened. In that moment he did not want to see the princess, but as he walked down the hallway he met her. He wanted to embrace her but before he did he turned and pointed to the stairs. The princess did not understand why he looked so upset, but she followed him quietly until they were at the top of the turret. Sandri turned and looked into the princess's eyes. He embraced her. With moist eyes he said, "There is only one day left for me in the fortress."

The princess stepped back a little and looked into his eyes. "I don't understand. Why are you leaving? What is happening?" She kept staring into those eyes of his and it felt to her like she was falling down. Slowly she sat down on the floor and Sandri sat beside her. Sandri felt deeply hurt inside. He did not want it to end like this, but he had no choice. For the next several minutes they just looked at each other with tears in their eyes. Then the princess raised her voice, and with trembling lips said, "Who wants you to leave? If my mother did this to you, I would never talk to her again."

"No, no," said Sandri as he looked straight into her eyes. "Today I completed my military term and now it is time for me to leave." He had no courage to tell her that the queen already knew about them, so he kept it secret.

The princess stood up angrily, and began to go inside without saying anything. Sandri remained in the turret not knowing what to do.

The next day Sandri went to the market. He wanted to buy something for the princess as a gift from him. He had never bought a present for a woman. He had no idea what to buy for her. After walking for two hours without buying anything, a couple yards away he noticed a woman sitting on a stone. She was looking at him. It was Zara, the woman who lived in an old hut on the flat top of the hill just a little bit outside the village of Bedolia.

In a loud voice she said, "Hello handsome boy. Do you have a girl that you love?"

Sandri with a wild glance said, "Might I know, why you are interested in knowing that?"

Zara said, "I have a beautiful flower. Maybe you can give it to her."

When he heard that she had a flower, he got even closer, and asked her, "Where is the flower? I don't see it anywhere. Can I see it?"

Zara stood up and said, "First you have to buy it. Then you can see it."

"Is the flower that expensive, that you won't allow me to see it?" ask Sandri.

It is very expensive, but if you decide to buy it, it is very cheap for you," said Zara.

Sandri sat on the stone where Zara had been sitting, to think for a few moments and said, "Yes I will buy it."

Zara approached the stone. Behind the stone, she had an old brown bag in which she had hidden the flower. She opened the bag and took out the flower saying, "Look at this. You may take it now"

Sandri started to laugh at her, and said, "This is not a flower, but only a stick set in a cup. Why are you calling it a flower?"

Zara smiled and said, "It will improve later on, and you will be surprised at how beautiful this flower becomes," and she directed it toward him. "The girl you will present it to will be happy."

"Ok. I will take your word that it will flourish later on. I believe you," he said.

"First I will tell you how to care for this flower. After it improves, do not allow anyone to see it, except you and your love that you will give it to. If anyone else sees it, it will dry quickly and will be as you see it now, and you will need to pass it to someone else as quickly as you can," said Zara.

Sandri took the flower and went back to the castle. He thought all day long about giving her this flower. He was feeling ashamed about it. He was saying to himself, "How can this be called a flower when there are no leaves on it. Maybe Artella will laugh at me when she sees it."

Later in the evening, he went to the princess's room to see her before leaving the castle. When he entered the room, he saw her on her bed. She was crying and upset about him needing to leave her.

Sandri approached her. "I'm here!" He said.

The princess's heart still palpitated every time she saw him. She opened her arms wide and embraced him. "I'm glad that you came to see me again. This is the last time we'll be together," said the princess as she laid her head on his chest. "Please, stay and hold me till morning as we end our love on this night."

"I would love to stay," said Sandri as he moved away a little from her. "I have a flower in this bag, and you are going to keep as a gift from me."

The princess arose from her bed and started walking from the window to the door and back again, she did not say a word.

Sandri turned his head toward her and said, "This flower comes from a strange woman who met me in the market. She promised me it would bloom later and bring you good luck."

The princess turned to him and wiped the tears from her face. She stooped and picked up the flower from him, and placed it on her windowsill. She looked at Sandri she said, "How lucky will I be when you go tomorrow. I will remain here alone with this flower that has no leaves. Perhaps with this stick, I will never forget you."

"Well, maybe, but you have to keep it safe, nothing can harm it, also do not allow anyone else to see it. I did not ask the woman at the market why you have to keep it that way, but just do it. Keep it safe," said Sandri.

They spent the night together, holding each other, weeping and kissing like never before. It was quiet until they heard a knock on the door, then they stirred awake. Sandri quickly fell to the floor behind the bed and held his breath for a moment. The princess stood up, gathered her white blanket underneath her arms and ran toward the door, but before she reached it the queen opened the door and came inside. The queen was afraid when she saw her daughter in front of her. "Why you are running my daughter?" the queen asked, as she looked stunned. The princess with heavy breathing said, "I just woke up mother, now I will dress and come eat breakfast with you."

The queen saw that her heart was pounding and asked, "My child, why are you afraid?

"Nothing mother," answered the princess.

The queen did not say anything more. She just a glanced at her and left the room, closing the door behind her.

Slowly Sandri got up from the floor. His face was dark with fear, and he quickly put on his clothes. The princess came near him and said, "You should go before my mother comes back."

"Yes, I'm going," said Sandri as he turned to face the princess.

They embraced each other for the last time. They kissed each other for a minute, and then broke it off.

"So you really think it's time for us to separate?" the princess said with tears in her eyes.

"Yes" he answered, "It will be better that way. I hope you will forget me very quickly."

Sandri never meant to hurt her. His heart felt the same way. He looked at her again and said goodbye, then stepped out of the room without looking back. She wanted to run after him but couldn't move. She felt sadness and knew that things had changed. Their love had ended.

# CHAPTER 4

Later that day, the queen came into the princess's room again. An awful look showed for a moment on her face when she saw her daughter still in bed. "Wake up. It is afternoon!" said the queen as she was standing next to the bed. "Are you going to sleep in all day and do nothing?"

The princess did not answer. She didn't feel like being with anyone at that moment. After what happened between her and Sandri, she did not want to speak with her mother or anyone anymore.

The queen sat beside the princess. When she looked at her she saw her red puffy eyes. Slowly she moved her hand over her daughter's head and ran her fingers through her hair. "What's wrong? Looks like you've been crying all day," she asked her.

The princess was sad and angry at the same time. She turned her grim face to her mother and said, "It's all right, mother. I will feel better later. I just want to be alone today." Then she closed her eyes and turned her face into her pillow and refused to talk anymore.

The queen knew why she was sad, but she couldn't say anything. She was silent and thoughtful for a moment. Then she got up and left the room.

As soon as she was gone, the princess pushed the covers back, slowly lifted herself off the bed and went to the window. As she was standing there looking out, one of her tears fell in the cup that was near her. She looked down and started laughing, although still feeling great sadness. Then in a soft voice she said, "If I could see Sandri again I would tell him that his flower has started to live."

She was happy when she saw a new leaf just starting to bloom. She could not wait to see how it would look with all of the leaves on it.

The next morning, when the princess awoke, she went to see her mother. She was trying to be strong like nothing happened, but the love was still in her heart just as strong as ever.

The queen began to feel a little more hopeful when she saw her daughter come to her room to spend time with her. Hopefully the situation would get better.

A week later the princess had a strange dream. She woke up feeling dizzy, tired and worse, but she thought it was nothing. While she was eating at the dinner table with her mother, she started to feel a little dizzy again. The queen asked carefully as she saw her touching her forehead, "Are you okay?"

"Yes, I am okay mother, just a little bit tired," said the princess as she closed her eyes for a moment. She then raised her hand and pressed it against her chest, trying to calm herself.

After several weeks, the princess went to the window. She pushed aside the curtains just a little. She looked down at the flower. It had become so beautiful with lots of new leaves. It had grown and changed so much that it had taken on the shape of a small tree.

She started to smile. Slowly she raised her right hand and touched one of the leaves that was close to her.

Immediately in that moment a strange feeling passed through her body. She knew that something was wrong. She stopped for a moment, and suddenly she touched her stomach. She felt something like a small rock inside it.

Her eyes grew wide and she froze for several moments as she struggled with her thoughts. She understood something that made her to feel pain deeply in her heart. She was pregnant.

In that moment she heard a loud knock at the door and almost fainted from the fear. When she opened the door, she saw the servant standing in front of her. She started yelling and with an angry tone she said, "I do not want anything; if I do, I will get it myself. I do not want to see you in my room again." She did not wait for the servant's reply and quickly shut the door.

The servant saw she looked upset, so took off immediately, without trying to explain that her mother wanted to speak to her.

The princess's first thought was that everyone would find out now what she was thinking. In those moments she felt like butting her head into the wall and ending her life forever. She knew that she would face the shame or poverty that would come to her very quickly. For her it was not just facing her mother, but all the people of her country. It was a terrible thing for her to discover. A sadness that she could not bear to think about.

After a few weeks of this, she began staying in her room. She did not have the courage to go and see her mother. She thought that if her mother knew she would punish her with death by hanging her before all the people.

In the imperial room, the queen was sitting on a chair beside the table, thinking something was suspicious. It had been a few days since she had seen her daughter. About that time, the servant came to bring lunch. The queen immediately asked her, "It has been a few days since I have seen my daughter. Have you been to her today?"

The servant bowed her head and said, "No, I have not seen her, your majesty. I don't know what happened to her, but she won't talk to me."

The queen quickly arose from the chair and left. She went straight into her daughter's room without knocking. She shook her head when she saw her still lying in bed. She looked at her for a moment and then walked around the bed toward her. "What is happening with you my daughter? Are you sick again?"

The princess did not answer; did not even raise her head or open her eyes to look at her.

The queen continued talking. "Okay, fine. I will go tell the servant and she can take care of you until you get well."

"No mother, I do not want anybody here," yelled the princess angrily.

"What are you angry about?" asked the queen.

"Nothing mother," said the princess. She wanted to tell her about her pregnancy, but she could not even look at her.

Every day she was lost in thought, wondering what to do with herself. During the night she could not sleep at all. The suffering in her heart did not allow her to sleep. In her mind she wanted to dismiss the secret one day and tell everyone that she was pregnant, but she could not do that, because it was such a terrible thing for her and everyone.

To forget her worries she walked in the yard but that started to turn out worse than she had imagined. The people she passed did not speak to her or even greet her. They considered her a sick and crazy person.

The queen worried every day about her daughter. She didn't know what was going on with her that caused her to not like anybody, even her. One day she decided to go and see her again. Before the queen reached the princess's room, the princess saw that she was coming. She returned quickly and went back to her room. She lied on the bed as if ill. Her face got remorseful whenever she saw her mother in her bedroom.

After a bit the queen came in and tried to speak with her. She also had a dress in her hands. She thought that maybe she would feel better when she saw it, but she didn't. She just became worse than she had been.

"I brought a dress for you to wear. Where should I put it? Should I hang it up in the closet?" the queen asked.

"No, leave it here," said the princess.

The queen stopped right where she was in front of her daughter's bed and said, "It is time for you to get out of bed and get ready to do something."

The princess did not speak for a few moments, and then said, "I do not want to see or talk to you anymore." Part of her loved her mother but another part hated her, because she was afraid of her.

The queen did not understand why she was sick but decided to leave her alone and not bother her again.

Several months passed. The flower was growing more and more and the princess's stomach grew much more than her clothes would cover. When she walked out of her room she wore a black cape so that no one could see her belly.

One morning, in the kitchen, there were three servants making breakfast for those who lived in the castle. When the kitchen door opened the servants were not surprised to see the princess standing before them. Slowly she started walking around the table trembling. She was afraid that maybe they could see her belly and they would tell everyone. "I want all of you out of the kitchen," she said.

The servants didn't understand what had happened to her. She used to be a friendly, helpful and very pleasant person but now she looked sick, sad and angry.

The servants did not say anything. They waved as they left, closing the door behind them. The princess remained in the kitchen looking at the food on the table, wanting to take some with her. She took a big bowl and filled it with many kinds of food. Then she left the kitchen and went straight to her room. She did this every day until one night when she had a dream. She dreamt that everyone knew her secret that she had kept since Sandri left. In that moment she screamed with a loud voice and then woke up. She was covered all over in sweat and pain had seized her stomach. She rose to her feet and began to walk across the room. She did not know what was happening to her. Her tears fell as rain and she could not stand the strong pain that came whenever she moved. She was trying to stop herself from screaming because someone might hear her. She quickly took a blanket and a gas lantern in her hand then slowly opened the door.

She went toward the red wall where the swords hung. She removed the right sword which unlocked the secret door and then pushed the wall which then swung open. Inside it was dark and scary. On one hand she was frightened to go in but on the other she had such pain that there was no other choice. She closed the door quietly behind her, locked it with the sword and headed to the last room, so nobody could hear her cry or scream from the pain. She entered the room holding the lamp before her, so she could see where she was putting her feet. Then she began to cry bitterly and loudly, and could not console herself. She pressed her back to the wall and slipped down until she was on the floor. She took a deep breath and then another. She was in a tough situation as there was no one there to support her while she was pushing but by the third push she had delivered her baby. Immediately the baby began to cry with a thin voice and trembling hands.

The princess had never had the experience of caring for a newborn baby. She was scared to take the baby in her hands but quickly covered the baby with a blanket. She saw that she had a boy but was not very happy. With her left hand touching his cheek, with a smile on her face, she said, "If I were married there would be great happiness that I had a prince, but in this case it would be a terrible mess for everyone if they found out."

After the painful experience that she had just been through she could not make up her mind about what to do with the baby. She was exhausted and fell asleep for little while.

It was midnight, a quiet night inside the castle where all were asleep, with only a soldier standing sentry on the top of the turret. It was also quiet in the secret room where the princess was sleeping. Her child slowly slid from her arms onto the floor and began crying loudly. The princess was startled and awoke. Quickly she took him in her arms and looked at him. The little boy wasn't crying because he was hurt but he was crying because he was hungry. The princess's dress had become wet from her breasts leaking milk. She thought immediately that she should feed him. Slowly she took out a breast and offered it to him. After she fed and covered him she spoke some kindly words to him. "I will try to make a life for you since you have come into this world, I will love you like all mothers who want their children and we will live together if we have a long life."

The lamp was going out little by little and barely illuminated the room so she had to go to her room to get another lamp. She slowly rose to her feet. She was in so much pain that she could barely move. She went to the door, opened it slowly then closed it behind her. After a few steps from the door she saw that the corridor had become light from the sun. She began to hurry so that she would be ready before the others woke up.

As she entered her room, her eyes went immediately to the flower that she had in her window. A beautiful white flower had just started to bloom. She looked at the flower and said aloud, "How strange is this flower! I will take it and put it near my son so that my son will never be alone." First, she walked through the room to see if she could find anything she needed. Quickly she took the blanket from her bed and spread it on the floor. She went to her closet and picked out some of her clothes and threw them onto the blanket as quickly as she could. With one hand she took the flower and lamp and with the other she folded the blanket with clothes into a ball and started to drag it to her son's room. Once there, she hurriedly set the lamp and flower on the floor, opened the blanket and began to rip her clothes one by one to make some small clothes and a small bed in the corner of the room. She felt guilty because she wouldn't be able to give him all the things that he deserved.

After a while she headed back to her room. Before her door had closed the queen entered. It was so strange that the queen had not had any conversation with her daughter for so long and today she felt very sad about that. The princess heard someone enter. She kept her eyes closed and tears squeezed through her lashes. "You are here, mother, aren't you?"

The queen slowly approached her, saying in a low voice, "I had to come here. It really hurts my heart to see you sick every day and not talking to anyone. Today something touched my heart and I felt very sad like never before." The princess could not stand in one place. She walked back and forth, looking at the queen. She paused for a moment and then she said, "What do you want from me mother?"

The queen looked at her sharply, "How can you ask me that? Every day I pray to God that someday you would recover and return to how you were before. I want you to join me for breakfast every morning and talk with me. That is what I want."

It was silent in the room for a moment and then the princess spoke.

"Yes, mother I will come, but I want you to leave me alone in my room, I do not want you to come in here, so tomorrow I will come to you."

The queen felt very happy. She hoped that her daughter would keep her word, so with a smile on her face she left the room and closed the door behind her.

The princess waited until her mother was away from the corridor and immediately left for the secret room. Once she had opened the secret door she saw a strange light coming from the room where she kept her son. She quickly ran toward the room and upon entering saw that the light was coming from the white flower that had bloomed! Shaking greatly, she quickly approached her child. She held him tightly in her arms and looked at the flower in amazement.

Every time she looked at that flower she saw something strange in it. It made her believe that this flower would help her raise her child. It was a strange plant which bloomed and shined only in dark places.

After several minutes she relaxed a little. She sat on the floor and began to speak to her son saying, "I will give you a present that you will keep forever. I give you the name of your father, who made me happy a year ago. We no longer see him, but with his name Sandri, we will remember him and we will never forget."

Even though she was afraid, she preferred to sleep in the secret room with her son every night and in the mornings go to her mother's room for breakfast. She thought that no one would notice.

# CHAPTER 5

Some months had passed by and little Sandri had grown. He was a beautiful boy, with a little face and big blue eyes, just like his mother.

He had begun crawling and no longer stayed in one place.

The princess felt bad for him, because she knew that he needed to go out sometimes, but she could not take him anywhere. She became concerned that she could not leave him alone in the room too long, because he would come out in the dark and get hurt when she was not there.

As she was thinking about what to do, suddenly her eyes went to the wooden box that was on the floor near a corner. She opened it rather slowly at first, and then she emptied it of the things that were inside. She put a blanket in the box and laid her son there. It was perfect to keep him safe, until he was old enough to understand that he could not leave the room.

One day, the princess was delayed with her mother. She was talking about how life has passed with the king, and how happy she was. The princess did not want to ask her anything. She was just listening to her. The queen was very pleased with her whenever she came to visit her. She tried to respect her more but never understood why she had such a feeling of sadness. She wanted to ask her, but she was afraid maybe Artella would become mad and never come to see her again.

As the queen was talking, the princess in her mind asked herself, "If I tell my mother about my son, what help would she give me, probably nothing, or she would kill me." In that moment she wanted to go because she knew that her son was awake from sleep and crying from hunger, so very quickly she rose from the chair and said, "I have to go now mother, I cannot be late anymore," and continued to walk out the room.

The queen rose from the chair and watching her said, "Yes, you can go now my daughter. We can talk again tomorrow," and she remained in the room silent.

On the way back from her mother's room, the princess started running in the long corridor as fast as she could. When she turned into the short corridor, she stopped and slowly entered her room. She was unable to open the secret door and to go to her son.

There were servants cleaning the floor of the corridor. They had blocked the way that the princess wanted to go. She waited and waited until the servants finished the cleaning. When they were gone, she went out of her room. She entered the secret door, but was surprised! The lighting was not glowing as usual from the last room, so something was not right. She rushed into the room as quickly as she could. The light of the flower was dim it could hardly make a shadow. Quietly she approached the wooden box and saw her son, who was lying down and not feeling well.

She shook him a little, but he didn't move or make a sound. She turned to face the tunnel door. She wanted to get him out of the room maybe that would help him a little. She gave the door a good push and it swung open.

She went back to the wooden box. With one arm she took her son and with the other, she took the flower, and went back in the tunnel. It was the first time that she had walked inside the tunnel but she didn't seem afraid at all. The tunnel was about six and a half feet tall and roughly square. It was built from stone on all sides, and was wide enough that three people could walk thru. It was very dark inside, but the light of the flower still lit a little and it was still light enough to see where she was going.

The queen was still confused in her room remembering the princess's words when she said that she did not want to be late. She rose several times from her chair and sat back down. She could not decide whether to go to her daughter's room to see why she was in such a hurry. Later she rose again, walked out of the room and through the corridor talking to herself saying, "I will go into her room even though she does not want me in there, I am going in." When she came near the princess's room, gently, she put her ear to the door, but heard nothing. She wanted to open the door but changed her mind. She turned and went back to her room.

After half an hour walking in the tunnel, the flower lost the light. The princess began to panic. The darkness surrounded her and she couldn't see anything.

After about a minute waking in the dark, ten yards away from her, she saw several lights coming through small holes so she started moving in their direction. When she reached there, it was a small door, which was closed with an iron. She put her son and the flower down on the ground and turned to open the door. She grasped the iron and pulled it very hard and the door burst open. She still could not get out of there. Some wild bushes had grown so high in the front that she could not see into the distance. She began to take them off one by one and finally she managed to see outside. She went back, took her son and the flower in her arms, and slowly passed by wild grass, which was all around the cave.

Twenty yards away from the cave was a river that was flowing from the high mountains, and some big, tall trees every two yards. There was a beautiful green meadow in front of the river and some small bushes by its edge.

She laid her son and the flower on the flat land near the river, and she stepped to the edge of the river on her knees. She made her hands into a fist and filled them with water, and made her son's face wet, so maybe he would open his eyes when he felt the water. She stood back to fill her hands again with water, and gave some to the flower too. She took her son and settled him in her lap while praying with all her soul and hoping that he would wake up soon. The rays of the sun warmed him little by little and the water on his face helped him to feel better. Leaves of the flower began to rise as they had been before. Little Sandri began to open his eyes occasionally.

Slowly he began to get better and better. He began to smile at his mother, and sneezed one time. She blessed him with tears streaming down her face. She smiled and kissed his head. From the day she learned that she was pregnant there was nothing good for her but after her son was born he was everything to her. She enjoyed the days with him. She did not want him to die but to live with her his whole life. She could not imagine her life without him.

Several months passed and little Sandri was now one year old. He had started walking. Every day he used to go close to the tunnel door and tried to open it. He cried for a long time sitting in front of the door. He wanted to go out. The princess could not get him out every time he wanted. She just waited until he stopped and fell asleep.

One afternoon, the princess wanted to change the bowl that held the flower. She thought that it was too small for the flower. Before she went to look for it, she put her son in the wooden box to stay until she returned. When she emerged from the secret room, she did not close the door. She thought that she would return soon. She went in the kitchen thinking she could find a bowl and return quickly downstairs.

The servants still left whenever the princess entered the kitchen and left her alone. As she was looking around the kitchen, she saw a bowl just past the edge of the table down on the floor, but before she picked it up, she saw a lot of food on the table. She thought to stop just for a little bit to eat. When she began eating, she forgot that she had left the door of the secret room opened.

The little Sandri had seen his mother go out of the room, so slowly he took off from inside the wooden box and got out of the room. In the distance he could see a light. He started walking toward the light, but he couldn't go very quickly because of the darkness and some small stones in the way. When he finally reached close to the stairs, he slowly moved his right foot to the edge of the first step, and then he crawled on his hands and knees like a baby bear. When he came to the top of the stairs, he grabbed the door and poked only his head in. He saw that there was a better room with more light that looked easier for him to move around in. He began to walk until he reached the long corridor leading to the royal room. By the door of the royal room there was a guard standing in front of it. Little Sandri went near the guard and began to smile with his thin lips. The guard smiled down at him, "Where are you going little child? Where's your parent?" he asked.

The little Sandri did not respond, he was not old enough to understand the words that the guard was saying, but he put a smile on his little face.

The guard wasn't thinking too much, he thought maybe he was one of those children who played in the yard, so he took him out and stood there with him.

As the guard was looking at the children, he noticed that the little boy did not belong with them.

All the children stopped playing and their eyes remained on little Sandri's clothes, which looked different than theirs. Their clothes looked well-made with good sewing, but little Sandri's looked ugly with one strip hanging around his shoulder, that held two pieces of material sewn by hand on both sides which were just about to fall from his body.

The princess was still in the kitchen. As she was eating, she heard a voice outside the kitchen. She stopped to listen. She heard a sound that made her heart stop and then beat wildly. Immediately she got up and went to the window. From the kitchen window she could see directly out to the yard. So when she looked outside her eyes went wide. She ran for the door and got out of the kitchen as fast as her legs could take her. She went to close the secret door.

It was getting dark outside, and all the children were gone. Only little Sandri was still there, no one took him. The guard grabbed little Sandri's hand and slowly went inside the castle directly to the queen. When he entered the room, the queen was near the window looking out of her room. He went close to her, bowed and said, "Excuse my boldness, I do not want to disturb you, but I do not know what to do with this child who was alone in the corridor."

"Why did you bring him here?" the queen asked the guard.

"I did not see anyone with him, and I sent him to the yard but no one took him. So I brought him here that maybe you would tell me what to do." said the guard.

"This is a strange situation," said the queen. She was surprised that someone would leave their own child. She turned back and went near the little child. "How is it possible for this child to enter this castle alone?" she asked the guard.

The guard had not seen anyone with him, and he did not know what to say to her, so he just remained silent.

The queen thought that someone had intentionally has left this child here, so she said to the guard, "I want to keep him here until morning. Go and call all the people to come by the front porch tomorrow morning."

The soldier bowed and said, "Yes, my queen," and left the room.

The princess was running down the corridor back and forth, but she couldn't see her son anywhere. A moment later she saw the guard who came from the royal room without her son. She was scared and wondering what was going to happen to her son. She went near the imperial room, and listened for a little bit by the door. She wanted to go inside but she thought that maybe it would be worse if she did. She was thinking in her mind that she would wait till he left the room and then catch him and run to the secret room. She waited for a while close to her mother's room without hearing anything until she heard her mother talking with her son. Then she heard her coming out. She quickly ran and hid around a corner and slid down on the floor, until her mother and her son passed.

She waited until they got through the corridor and had reached the kitchen, but she remained in the corner, broken, not knowing what to do.

When the queen with the little child entered the kitchen, the servant stopped and looked at them spuriously.

Little Sandri smelled the food. He began to walk slowly and approached the table that was laden with food on the top. He raised his hands trying to touch the table but he could not, it was higher than he was. The queen started laughing aloud while looking at him. She said to the servant, "Give a cup of milk to this little boy."

The servant, without saying anything, went to the cabinets and opened them. She took a cup and filled it with milk and fell to her knees in front of him saying, "Here, take this and drink. This is good."

He took the cup with both hands and began to drink as he never drank before, but it was true that he did not drink milk before. He was so hungry that he did not stop until he completed all the milk in the cup.

The queen was looking at his clothes, which were all dirty and strange looking. She addressed the servant and said, "Take the child, clean him up, and bring him fresh clothing. When you finish, bring him to my room."

The princess stepped forward from the corner then started walking toward the kitchen. The door stood open and she tried to listen very closely, but she could not hear anything other than her mother's whispers to the servant.

A few moments passed and then the queen came out of the kitchen. She met the princess just by the door and asked her very slowly, "Where have you been my daughter?"

The princess trembled and was unable to speak with her mother because of the fear and shame that she felt. She rolled up her eyes and looked away so the queen could not see her face. With a deep groan, she said, "Nowhere mother, I was only outside."

The princess was acting like she was going crazy, so the queen didn't have courage to tell her about the child that was in the kitchen. She said in her mind, "If I tell her she might become furious. It would be better to leave her alone."

Both of them began to walk in opposite directions. The queen went in the direction of the long hallway to go to her room, and the princess in the direction of her room, but she couldn't glance back to make sure that her son was still in the kitchen, so she kept her head down and went to her room.

Shortly after the servant finished her job, fed and cleaned little Sandri, she sent him to the queen.

When the queen saw the boy with those clothes, she laughed and said, "Those clothes are too big for you, but don't worry tomorrow we will find your parents and we will help them buy you some better clothes."

Little Sandri was just smiling. He felt good after he had been cleaned and fed. He looked so cute, with his big blue eyes and brown hair which was curly at the ends. He looked just like her daughter, but she couldn't think of that. He began to enter into the queen's heart. She began to like him as if he was her grandson.

She took him and put him on her bed, and kissed him on his cheek, then said to him, "I think you are tired now, so you have to sleep on my bed tonight."

Little Sandri was very happy with a smile on his face. He bounced on her bed until he got very tired and fell asleep.

The queen was awake all night talking to herself saying, "If I had a grandchild like him to hold in my arms and hug I would be very happy. I think I will never see this miracle in my life. With the mind of my daughter's, it will never happen."

# CHAPTER 6

The princess wept while walking back and forth all night, but not a sound did she hear in the long hallway as she waited. She felt pain in her body since she had been awake all night. Her eyes were red and sore so she could barely see. She thought she had lost her son forever.

She wanted to sneak into her mother's room so many times that night, but she could not go in, because outside the door a guard stood watching.

When morning came the princess was still walking with her feet aching from fatigue. Sometimes she put her face to the window of the corridor, looking at a large number of people who had gathered by the front porch of the castle, covering the yard like leaves that fall in autumn. She did not know why they had come, but in her mind she thought her mother was doing something with her son.

At the queen's room a soldier knocked at the door. Slowly he came in, as he bowed and said, "Excuse me your majesty, all the people have come and they are waiting for you."

The queen was sitting next to the little boy on the bed, and watching him, how well he was sleeping. Slowly she stood up, walked across the room, stared down at the floor and said to the soldier, "You can go, and I will be prepared to come out in a moment."

The soldier went out closing the door behind him.

The queen slowly went over to little Sandri. She sat down on the bed, patted him through the blanket, and slowly said, "Can you wake up little boy?"

Little Sandri started to move little by little and raised his hands to wipe his eyes. When he opened his eyes, he started to cry a little, because he did not see his mother in front of him, but a strange woman looking at him.

"Are you afraid of me?" The queen asked as she smiled at him and said, "I am going to give you a cup of milk that I brought for you, so do not cry." She tried to get him to drink milk, but he refused. He turned his head away from her. He was afraid to look back. He seemed to be shy at that moment.

"Don't be afraid," said the queen in a soft voice as she picked him up, and sat him down on the floor, "Give me your hand and we will walk out together." She did not want to let him go but was she also concerned that someone might be looking for him.

Before little Sandri gave his hand to the queen, he ran and caught her dress. He tried to hug her legs, but with his small arms he could not reached all the way around. The queen glanced down at the little boy who was still hugging her legs. She fell to her knees and put her hands on the sides of his face and said, "If no one claims responsibility for you, I will take you and keep you as my child and I will make you a prince of the state." In her heart she felt something, but her mouth could not speak.

As the princess stood in the corridor looking out the window, she heard the door open from her mother's room. She began to run and went into hiding in the corner. Then her mother and her son passed her in the corridor. When she saw them together, she burst into tears, but did not dare to move.

The queen walked out to the front porch landing toward her chair. She put little Sandri on another chair nearby her. She turned and said to the people, "Listen carefully, please. This little child was found within the castle, and please if he is yours come and get him." Then she stopped. She waited about a minute, but no one moved. Everyone looked stunned. Slowly she went back to her chair and sat. She was in a very bad position since no one came to claim the little boy.

Inside the castle the princess was watching from the window. She did not know what she could do to help her son that she longed to hold so badly. She could not bear it any longer. Slowly she came out and stood silently behind her mother's chair. She stood there and was prepared to stay put for a while. As little Sandri lifted his head up a little, he saw his mother.

Immediately he began to cry. The poor child cried until he was quite out of breath. He tried to get down from the chair he was sitting on. He turned, supported his chest on the chair, and tried to touch the ground with his little feet. At that moment, the princess took a deep breath. Her body was shaking as she started walking toward her son, and walked past her mother without a sound. She picked her son up and embraced him. She had missed him so much. With joy, little Sandri cried even more. He tightened his arms around her neck, pressing so close like he had not seen her for a long time.

"What are you trying to do? Leave him on the chair!" The queen said in a hard voice without rising from her chair.

The princess stopped. "The child is mine," she answered. It was not something she liked to admit in that way, but she could not deny the pain in her heart any longer.

The queen was stunned as she heard her daughter. With an angry face she said, "Leave him on his chair please. You are still sick."

However, the princess did not wait for her mother to rise from the chair. At first, she turned around to see if someone was in front of her, and then she whispered as she began to run inside the castle with her arms wrapped around her son. She ran like a gazelle through the corridor and entered the secret room. As the door clicked closed behind her, she was surprised with herself, being able to remain hidden in the secret room again.

After the princess left, the queen quickly rose to her feet and turned to General Drof and with a slight movement of her head said, "You come with me," as she went inside of the castle, leaving behind the trailing sound of the people who did not understand.

"Yes," Drof answered as he walked after her.

The servants went all over the castle but they could not find her anywhere. The long corridor was empty with no sign of the princess. The queen and Drof rounded the end of the hallway and they went from room to room until they came to the princess's room where Drof burst open the door. As soon as they entered the room, the queen stood with open eyes. She stood there for a moment in kind of a shock. She began walking slowly around the room staring at the empty bed surprised! Now she understood why her daughter hadn't allowed anyone to come into her room. At that point, she began to believe that the little boy was her daughter's child.

Her first thought was that the servants would have seen her or known something about this, so immediately she turned to Drof and said, "Go and call all the servants to the imperial room to meet with me." Drof immediately went. A few moments later the servants came into the imperial room. The queen began to speak and ask them, "What can we do to find her? How is it possible for her to have kept that child here secretly without anyone seeing them, if that child is hers?"

However, no one spoke, because no one had seen the princess or anything strange like that. They had seen her sick, but they never thought she was hiding a child.

Drof was beside the queen with his hands behind his back. He stepped forward and raising his voice said, "She has fled from the castle, so we'll never find her."

The queen turned her head toward him, "My daughter was not all right, as far as we knew. We are not sure whether the child is hers or not. And you, how do you know this?"

"Perhaps you don't trust me. She fled because she could not stay here after her foolishness. She did not follow the rules," said Drof.

"No!" the queen spoke as she shook her head ruefully. "This is not the time to talk about what she did, but to find her. She disappeared from the castle without telling me anything. In some ways, I think she may have made contact with the guard Sandri who worked here two years ago, or it could be she has friends none of us know about. Who could they be?"

"Yes. I remember him," said Drof, "After the death of the king, the princess did not talk to anyone, just with him. She used to stay all day with him in the yard, inside the castle, everywhere sitting together, but I never thought that she would do something with him. He was just a guard, no more than that, who was at the front door sometimes."

As the queen was walking toward the window, she paused and said, "Every day I was wondering, why she was so sad when I saw her. Perhaps I didn't really understand her. I asked her many times what was bothering her, but she never ever told me. Why didn't she say anything?"

Everybody was disappointed, but no one was more disappointed than the queen.

"I must find Sandri. He would help me find my daughter. I want him here. I'm not exactly sure how you can find him, but I need to see him!" she declared.

"Yes. Your majesty, I will try to find him and I won't come back without finding him," said Drof as he left the room with the others.

In the secret room that awful morning, little Sandri pressed his face into his mother's shoulder and wept for a long time. He was tired and just wanted to nestle in his mother's arms. The princess had already made up her mind to leave the castle and to go somewhere far away where no one could find her. She did not want to leave her home but was worried and thought that her mother was going to kill her and her son.

After a while she rose to her feet and pushed open the tunnel door. She took the flower and put it in the same brown bag that Sandri gave to her. Also she took some of the things that her father had left in the room and put them in the other bag. She thought that maybe she could sell and use them for living somewhere.

She started walking in the tunnel, but the things that she made ready to take with her, she could not carry, because they were too heavy and she knew that she could not make it to the end. So she dropped them on the floor and continued walking with just her son and flower in her hands.

# CHAPTER 7

Toward the middle of the day, there was still no sign of the princess in the castle. The queen was so sad that she thought her heart would break waiting in the imperial room for something to happen. So she went out of the room, and slowly made her way down the hall, passing door after door. When she had reached the princess's bedroom door she entered, shutting the door behind her. Tears filled her eyes, as she felt guilty about the time she had spent away from her daughter. She didn't think anything like this could have happened. She was standing in silence, alone in the room, and was just staring at the wall thinking about everything. Suddenly she looked down. She saw the dust all over the floor. She paused, unsure of what was going on. She began to walk out of the room as she followed the dust. But when she came close to the wall with the red tiles the trail ended. She looked up. She saw the sword on the right side and the gas lamp, that were hanging on the wall were missing. She looked down again. When she looked closer in front of the wall, on the floor she could see in the dust the footmarks from where the princess had walked in and out. She couldn't believe her eyes, and then she stared at the wall again. Slowly she started touching it with both hands and then ran her fingers across the red tiles. She could clearly see small cracks on three sides of the wall in the shape of a door.

She pushed the wall, but nothing happened. She pushed it again, and heard something had moved. She stopped and put her ear to the wall and listened, but she heard nothing. The noise that she heard was from the sword that was hanging in the iron on the other side of the wall, and kept the door locked. So every time she pushed the wall, the sword moved. She knew that something was holding it and she couldn't open, but she kept pushing until she heard a loud noise and the door burst open. Her eyes, as she looked inside, were wide open. It was so quiet and dark that she couldn't see anything. She turned around and ran through the corridor toward the kitchen and went in. She grabbed a lamp from the table next to the door, lit it, and went back to where she had been. Slowly she entered the secret place and stood there, just inside the open wall. With one hand she raised the lamp and held it high so she could see, and with the other on her chest, she thought her heart might fail her. Slowly she stepped down on one stair and stopped, listening for a few seconds, but she heard nothing. Before she took the next step, she called the princess's name, but no response. So she continued walking down the stairs, a couple of steps down she saw a room to the right side. She stepped inside and looked, but it was only full of dust and spiders. Slowly she moved forward. She saw another room that was also empty, but when she reached the last one, she was shocked for a minute and then she started looking all over the room. She saw a pile of clothes on the floor in the corner, a bedspread, pillow and wooden box, all those things she recognized, but none of the treasure that was lying on the floor by the tunnel door. She set the lamp down and knelt by the wooden box. She grabbed the blanket and pressed it against her chest. Now she understood why her daughter was acting so hostile and angry at her, but she didn't understand why the king and her daughter kept this place secretly.

Meanwhile, the princess was walking alone in the scary darkness of the woods without seeing any houses or any paths. She was already exhausted, so she sat motionless on the ground by some bushes, holding her son tightly to her chest under her cape. She was so terrified to stay in that darkness, because she had never been in the forest before. She was very hungry. She did not bring any food or water with her. For her son, she had breast milk, but if she did not eat something, her breasts would soon dry up, and her son would cry until he ate something.

In the middle of the night, the princess was still awake. She tried to sleep, but she was frightened that wild animals would soon come and eat them. She stayed sitting there quietly, trembling from head to foot, while staring into the darkness around her. Several times, she thought she saw and heard something close to her, and it made her heart beat like a drum. She closed her eyes fitfully and suddenly when she opened her eyes again her heart stopped. A couple yards away from her, she saw the yellow eyes of many wolves glowing around her, and they wanted to eat her. Slowly she reached her hand and grabbed a thick branch that was nearby her, and held it in front of her. She knew that she couldn't fight off so many of them, and couldn't run or scream. She could not do anything. She just closed her eyes, so that she could not see the wolves attack her. Slowly one of the wolves came near her and opened his huge mouth with sharp teeth trying to bite her, but in that moment the flower broke the bag and with a big ray hit the wolf in his eyes and the wolf ran away with the others. When she opened her eyes again, the wolf was no longer in front of her. She couldn't believe she had survived. She stayed there under the bushes, scared, worried and frightened and later she fell asleep.

Toward morning, as little Sandri stretched his arms the princesses awoke.

She was so cold and tired that she was barely moving. She forced herself back onto her feet, and headed deeper into the forest. She had no idea where she was or which direction to take, she only knew that she had to keep moving. She was worried she was going in a circle and would come to the same spot that she was before. Her heart was not quiet since she had come this way. Her breath was coming heavily now as she walked, she knew that she would collapse soon if she didn't eat something. Little Sandri was crying from hunger and thirst, but the princess could do nothing. She just kept walking in the heavily wooded forest, hoping that she would find a house soon.

After she had walked for several hours, she came to a place where she heard water gurgling somewhere nearby. She needed a drink so badly. As she went near, she saw the river. A few yards away she saw an old bridge, which was built of wood. She was so happy when she saw it. She thought there would be a path after it. There was a very big tree and bushes close to the bridge. It seemed that no one had used it for a long time.

As she passed the tree, she saw that many pillars of the bridge had rotted from water that had gone high and covered them. She was wondering what would happen if she fell in the water and no one was there to help. She started walking slowly, but stopped for a moment and looked at the ripples of the water that made her heart thump. She began to walk again, first with the right foot and then her left foot without stopping. Then a few inches in front of her feet, one of the pillars was rotten. When she came to step on it there was a loud crack. She fell, into deep water, together with her child and the bag. The water entered her mouth and she was swallowing, choking and gasping for air. Then she dipped under the water again. After much struggling, finally, she burst out of the water, dragging herself to shore. She had managed to survive somehow with her son in her arms, but the bag slipped from her hand and was swept away by the water.

She put her son on the meadow by the river, and wiped the hair from his face. She thought he was choking, but little Sandri smiled wide. No water was in his mouth. She started laughing and crying, hugging and kissing him on his cheeks, then she went back into the water. She continued to look through the water, but she could not see the bag, only the river going on as far as she could see. Her eyes got wide and she backed away saying "No, no." She started to panic. She knew that she needed the flower she had in the bag to survive.

After a little bit more searching, she saw the bag was stopped by the branches of a tree. Quickly she ran out of the water. She began to run on the edge of the river until she got near the tree. She tried to get the bag but she could not reach it. She turned and went over to the tree. Slowly she lay down on the tree's branch that was out over the water. With one hand she held onto the branch and with the other hand she grabbed the bag, but at that moment, she heard a creak and the branch broke. She fell into the water again. She could not swim anymore. She had lost her strength and could not move anymore. She just held the flower tightly in her arms. She remained in the water and sunk to the bottom, but in a very short time something caught her on the back of her dress and pulled her out of the water.

After a little bit the coughing and sputtering had ended and she was able to see who had saved her. It was an old woman with many wrinkles on her face, holding a stick that had a hook on the tip. For the old woman it was not the first time she had saved a life. She had used it to save her lambs so many times before and for that reason she carried that long stick with a hook.

After the woman saved the princess from the water, she tried to find out what she was holding between her hands that she ran after and risked her life for. So she went close to the princess and said, "I saw you were holding on that branch, but I was too late to catch you. I ran behind you, but the branch didn't hold you until I arrived."

The princess could hardly breathe. She could not speak. She closed her eyes for a couple seconds then she slowly got up and began to run straight to her son. She reached down, hoisted him into her arms and sat down on the grass.

She had traveled so long in the forest without meeting anyone, so she was so happy to see a woman in front of her, helping her.

At first the princess asked the woman, "Do you have something for us to eat? I haven't eaten anything for two days."

The woman said, "Of course I will give you the bread that I have, and for this little boy I will milk a sheep and give him some milk. I think he is too young to eat the bread."

The woman reached inside of her old bag, pulled out a cup and a piece of bread, "Eat this, it will help," she said.

The princess took the bread and began to eat it, holding it with both hands. Little Sandri with his little hands wanted to take the bread from his mother's mouth. He knew that she was eating something good.

Immediately the princess broke a little piece of bread and gave it to him.

He ate as if he had all his teeth in his mouth. It tasted so good that he wanted more.

The woman quickly milked a sheep and came back with a cup of milk, and gave it to little Sandri. He was so happy that he could not wait to drink it.

The princess said to the woman, "You saved our lives and God will make you very happy."

The woman said, "I'm glad you survived for your child and now don't worry, just take a rest, and tell me where you are going."

The princess did not say anything but just kept silent. She did not know what to say to her. The woman stopped and did not speak. She understood that she was tired and did not want to talk, but later she asked her again, "Where are you going, do you have somewhere to go or maybe you need help or something?"

The princess did not want to tell her about what had happened in her life. It was so hard for her to talk about her past. She could not tell anything to the woman. "I'm a simple woman with a child in my hands all alone and I don't know where to go, I lost everything I had before," then tears fell from her eyes. She used to cry every day, not because she was sad, but because she could not tell the secret to anyone and make her life easier. It was the sad truth.

The woman saw that she was sad about something, and said to her, "Don't worry, you will come with me. You will live in my house until you find what you lost. I do not know what you had, a house or anything else but I will help you and your son. I have an old small house but it does not matter because you need help."

The princess thanked her very much because she did not have anything else and maybe that woman would help her to find a new life.

It had been a long time since the princess had spoken to anyone besides her son. She really missed talking with someone and spending the day happy. She cried from happiness because she really needed the help.

Before darkness fell the woman said to the princess, "Now is time to go because we have a long way to walk, and it's better to go earlier."

The woman took the blanket, put it on the small carriage, and said to her, "You can put your child here and I can pull it, it is a little small but it works."

The princess trembled when the woman wanted to take her son from her hands. She opened her eyes and said, "I will hold him because I am fine now."

The woman looked at her with surprise and said, "Ok, but give me that bag to carry for you."

The princess shouted with a high voice, "No, no I will carry it too, don't worry about me."

"I just wanted to help you. I don't want to see you upset," said the woman.

The princess felt badly that she had spoken loudly to her and said, "I'm sorry, I'm a little bit sick and sometimes I don't know what I'm saying." Then she put her head down.

"You can call me Melli if you want," the woman said as she walked away, went to gather her sheep and to start going.

Melli and the princess went down the mountain. They passed the forest and approached the hill. Down the hill, was a small and old house built from wood and spattered with mud all around. It was the only house close to that hill.

The house had two small rooms inside and each of them had a window and between them was an old door just about to fall down. In the front yard there was a small shed made with thick branches that Melli called the cattle shed.

After Melli put her sheep in the cattle shed she turned and said to the princess, "I have lived in this house for so long all by myself, so it is nice to have company. Don't be afraid, no one is within."

When Melli opened the door, the princess stopped on the threshold, and started looking at the room, but she was not surprised. It was not the worst room that she had ever seen before. She lived for one year worse than this, but she was looking to see if she could find a place to hide the flower, so Melli couldn't see it.

The room was small with a low ceiling and the floor was just bare earth. In a corner of the room was a bed made of wood covered with straw with an old blanket on the top of it. There was a little wooden stool by a little wooden table close to the chimney that was black from the smoke. There were some foot-long strips of dry meat hanging against the wall. On the opposite side from the chimney was a door as large as a person. That was another room.

Melli, from the time she met the princess, knew there was something wrong going on, but she could not ask her yet. She grabbed the princess's hand and said, "Come, don't be afraid. My house is not big enough, but you can sit here on this stool or you can go into the next room first if you want to look in it."

The princess started walking directly toward the next room. She opened the door slowly. It was a small room with only an old bed in the corner of the room. She wanted to put the flower somewhere in the room, but there was nowhere to hide it other than next to the bed. As she got down on her knees, she quickly opened the bag and looked inside to see what had happened to the flower, taking a big risk in taking it out. The white flower that was making the light was snapped, but she did not worry too much because her son was feeling well and the leaves were still strong. She covered the flower again and put it in the corner of the room next to the bed and very quickly got out of the room. She sat on Melli's bed without a smile.

Melli was looking at her. She knew that she had hidden something in the room but she did not want to ask her about it.

# CHAPTER 8

On the day that the princess had disappeared the soldiers went from village to village looking for her and Sandri, and they found nothing out about them. The next morning soldiers arrived at the market hoping to get some news from there about Sandri.

People came and went, but no one told the soldiers anything about Sandri, except a young boy who stood still and looked at them for a moment. He was wearing some dirty old clothes and an old ripped up hat. It was Lanti, who was now 13 years old. He slept in any corner he could find on the street just in front of the market. During the day he tried to help anyone he could so he could get something to eat. His father, Sorne, died a year ago and a short time later his mother, Zara, also died. So he was left alone with no family to care for him.

He heard the soldiers say they were looking for Sandri. Slowly he went close to them and said, "I know who you are looking for. Sandri, right?"

Drof heard him saying Sandri's name and immediately turned and said, "We have been looking for him out here because we know he is here somewhere, and I wanted to see him. Please tell me where I can find him?"

"Tell me first why you need him and I will tell you where he is," said Lanti.

Drof approached him and said, "I will give you a gold coin if you tell me!"

Lanti was thinking at first and said, "I want to see the golden coin first and then I will tell you."

Drof put his hand in his jacket, and pulled out a small black bag that was full of coins. He took one golden coin from it and with an open hand showed it to him.

When Lanti saw the golden coin, he took his hat from his head. He put the tip of the hat in his mouth and started chewing from the surprise, looking at a coin that he had never held before in his own hands. He reached out his hand to pick it up, but Drof closed his hand very quickly and said, "No, no, first you have to tell me where he is, and after that you can have it."

Lanti started talking with a loud voice and said, "Sandri comes here to the market every day and maybe he will come again today."

One of the soldiers said to Drof, "Do you really believe this boy, he's obviously lying." "This boy won't go anywhere till we find what we are looking for," said Drof and he caught Lanti by his jacket. "I will hold you like this until you tell me the truth."

Lanti became scared and very quickly said, "Ok, ok, I will stay with you here until you find him."

Yes Lanti was telling the truth. Sandri did come every day to the market. He lived and worked at somebody's farm, in a village near the market. After leaving the castle two years ago, it was very difficult for him to find a place to live, but after many days he finally met a man that needed help on his farm. He worked hard every day to make his living. So after a while as the soldiers were waiting Sandri showed up. He was wearing some dirty old clothes and was holding a little lamb in his arms. He had no idea that someone was looking for him so he had a little smile on his face and looked like he was happy about something.

When Lanti saw him, he started screaming loudly and said, "You're looking for this man right?" The soldiers ran immediately and grabbed Sandri's hands from both sides.

Lanti said to Drof, "Can I have the coin now?"

"Yes. You can have it now, your work is finished," said Drof he threw the coin to the ground.

Lanti reached down and picked up the coin. He was looking at it with a happy face, but that did not last long. By the time he had straightened up again the soldiers had tied Sandri's hands without saying a word.

Sandri began to talk to them, "Leave me alone, why are you taking me?"

Lanti ran and began to argue with the soldiers, "Why are you taking him, leave him alone please, why are you taking him?" He argued with Drof, "Here take your coin. I don't need your coin." He threw it in Drof's face and he tried to push them away from Sandri, but they pushed him and knocked him to the ground.

Sandri had no clue where or why they were taking him, but he said to Lanti, "Take this lamb and keep it till I come back."

"Yes. I will wait for you," said Lanti and he remained in the market holding the lamb by the rope with his eyes full of tears.

After a time, the soldiers arrived in the castle yard. They were on their horses and had a rope tied around Sandri's hands, pulling him like an animal.

The queen heard that the soldiers were back so she went immediately to the yard.

When she saw Sandri it seemed more likely that she would eventually see her daughter again. She felt very happy and could not wait to talk with him because she thought he would help her find her daughter.

She got very angry when she saw the soldiers had tied him. She went near them and said to Drof, "Untie his hands immediately."

The soldiers looked at her with surprise. They were expecting her to thank them, but she did not like what she saw and felt sorry for him.

Drof dismounted his horse and said to the queen, "Why do you want to release this thief? He is the cause of this problem we are having now and you want to release him?"

"Don't make me speak again, do as I say," said the queen.

"You can tell just by looking at him that he is hiding something from us," said Drof.

"Do as I say," the queen exclaimed.

Drof did not say anything else. He untied Sandri's hands as he watched him like a hawk.

"Come with me," said the queen to Sandri.

Sandri continued to walk behind her followed by Drof. When the queen noticed that Drof was still with them she did not like it. She turned and said, "Leave us."

Drof did not want to turn back. He wanted to know what she would say to Sandri but he had to do as the queen said so he turned back.

The queen and Sandri entered the imperial room. The queen walked around the room. She wanted to ask him so many questions but somehow she could not say a word. There was silence in the room for a minute. The queen moved toward Sandri where he stood by the door confused. She placed her hands on his shoulders and spoke quietly. "I'm not trying to punish you, but I'm trying to find out what happened to my daughter and I thought you would help me find her and her child."

Sandri did not understand what the queen was talking about. Several things went through his head, but he was surprised and he could not even ask exactly how princess Artella could be missing. He did not know anything about her, even whether she had a child, because he had not seen her for two years. However, he had to say something to the queen, "I don't have any answers for this my queen."

The queen thought for a little bit while looking at him and said, "You are the only one that knows where she went. I think you helped her disappear from the castle."

"No, no," said Sandri and he put his head down. He felt much more embarrassed than scared.

"After the king died my daughter didn't talk to anyone accept you, and after you went from the castle she appeared to be mentally ill, so tell me the truth now."

Sandri did not have the courage to say anything to her, because he did not know what would happen to him after he told her that he had slept with her daughter. He became beet red embarrassed and felt his mouth running dry. He tried to tell her the truth that he had not seen the princess for a long time but the queen didn't believe him. The queen made her way to the door. As she opened it, she saw Drof was already by the door listening. He jumped in fear when he saw the queen. Immediately he said, "What punishment do you want to prepare for him? My queen."

Waving a finger she said, "Put him in prison," and walked away. She felt sorry for him, but she knew that he was the father of her daughter's child. So she thought it was best to just let him tell the truth in his own time.

Sandri was waiting in the imperial room and thinking, "If I'm the father of her child it was a big mistake that I never came to see her." At that moment Drof and two soldiers came toward him. They grabbed him, bound his hands and took him away from the imperial room. They got through the castle corridor and they reached the stairs of turret. The small door just down the stairs was the door of the prison.

Sandri immediately knew where they were taking him. He knew every inch of the castle. He started talking with them, "What are you doing with me now? Where are you taking me?" He tried to run but he could not. The soldiers were holding him too tightly so he could not move. Drof opened the door and they entered the prison. After the bottom of the stairs there were three doors with small windows on them. Drof unlocked the door that was closest to the stairs and pushed Sandri into the room. The floor of the room was just dirt and it had only a small window that could allow the entry of two or three rays of the sun. Before Drof shut the door he said to him, "We are keeping you in prison, but don't ever think to tell the queen anything because she could take your head off," and he slammed shut the door.

Drof did not want to find the princess anymore. He thought that the only person close to the queen now was him and, in his mind, he wanted something from the queen.

He had tried to make her fall in love with him, thinking that someday he would be king, but the queen never accepted his advances.

# CHAPTER 9

It was a chilly morning. The wind blew trailing smoke from the chimney of the old, small, quiet house in the forest. Inside the princess spent her first night with her son and felt safe after she had faced near death. She would have died if it hadn't been for Melli helping her and offering her a place to stay.

The princess woke up and smelled the fragrance of fresh bread. Slowly she rose from the bed and went to find where the smell was coming from.

Melli was near the chimney. She had already built a fire in the fireplace and cooked for them before they awoke then made it ready to eat.

The princess, with a smile on her face, said to Melli, "I missed that smell of fresh baked bread. You have a kind heart." She had not finished her words when little Sandri opened the door and came out of the room.

As he walked slowly, blinking and rubbing his eyes, he stopped near Melli. He looked at her, because he knew that she would give him something to eat. Melli and the princess started laughing when they saw him stop because he looked like a little puppy.

"The little boy has also smelled baking bread," said Melli as she helped him sit on the wooden stool. She then fell to her knees in front of him, "Here, take this cup of warm milk and drink, this is good. Be careful, you don't want to burn your mouth."

After a short silence Melli, as she looked at the princess's eyes said, "I couldn't ask you yesterday for your name, I saw that you were too tired to talk, so tell me what your names are?"

The princess could not tell her true name because Melli would know who she was, but she said half of her name, "You can call me Tella and my son is called Sandri," then she turned her head as her face went dark.

Melli did not recognize that she was the princess. She hadn't seen her since she was a little girl.

After they finished eating, Melli said to the princess, "I will go to the market. I'm taking two sheep with me to sell there. Maybe I will be lucky and sell them because I need to make a living."

"Is the market far from here?" the princess asked.

"For my age it is far so I walk slowly but it won't be too late when I return. So you stay here and don't be afraid. You have seen that no one comes to my house. It's only my house here."

"No, I will not be afraid. I will stay and wait until you come back," said the princess.

So Melli went out of the house, took two sheep from the cattle shed and headed to the market.

Every time Melli went to the market she had to carry the sheep for miles. She had to pass through the forest of tall trees. It took an hour for her to get there.

After Melli had arrived at the market with her two sheep, two soldiers from the kingdom suddenly came and faced her. One of them held a sword in front of her face. The other rushed to take one of her sheep and said to her, "One sheep is enough for you to sell today, so get lost now."

Melli did not say anything to them, because she was accustomed to them. She turned around slowly and started to walk away from them with her head down. She felt so sad but there was nothing she could do.

They were many people at the market walking back and forth. It seemed that it was a very busy day which was good for Melli and she sold the sheep immediately.

She was happy but she did not want to go back home with empty hands for the little boy. So she bought some small cloths for him and a dress for the princess. She was excited to go back home and show what she bought them. Suddenly as she was walking she heard some people saying something strange! "Princess Artella went lost two days ago. She took a little boy with her!"

Melli immediately turned back and looked at them. She heard every word they were saying. She stopped for a moment before saying anything to them. She started thinking for a little bit but was not sure whether to speak. Should she tell them about the woman that she had in her house or be quiet until she finds the truth for herself. In that moment she could not move her mouth to say anything to them or to ask any questions so she just walked away slowly toward her house. The path seemed to be much longer than before. Every time she took a step on the way home she asked herself, "I didn't think she was telling me the truth. How can I find the truth?"

At the old house in the forest it was very quiet. Little Sandri was sleeping on Melli's bed on his stomach with his hands up around his head. The princess was worried that something bad had happened to Melli. She stayed inside by the window, because she couldn't go to look for her, and waited for her to return.

After thinking long and hard while walking, finally Melli reached the house. When she approached the door, she stopped. From the feeling that she had, she could not open the door. First, she took a deep breath, raised her hand to push the door, but in that moment, the princess opened the door from the inside and said, "I'm so glad you are back, I was so worried about you."

Melli's face was so dark and bluish. She could not say anything to her. She just walked directly to her bed and sat on it. She took a breath again and said to the princess, "I bought some clothes for you and for your son, here take them."

The princess immediately realized that something had happened at the market so she asked her, "Are you feeling all right?"

"I just had a hard day and I need my rest," answered Melli.

The princess started walking in a circle and could not stay in one place. She stopped and got near to Melli's bed and she asked her again, "Please tell me what happened at the market."

Melli thought for a minute, and turned to her, "You want the truth?"

"Yes. I want the truth," said the princess.

"Some soldiers took one of my sheep so I couldn't sell both of them," said Melli while watching her.

"Why would they do that?" asked the princess.

"They do that because they have to feed the kingdom. They don't pay anything. They just take things from the poor people."

The princess put her head down and looked at the floor. She felt ashamed, but there was nothing she could do or say.

After a while, little Sandri woke up. The princess took him and started taking off his old clothes. She then put on the new ones that Melli had bought for him.

It was a grey jacket with two buttons on the front that reached to his ankles. It was old but fit well and was so nice. He could also walk easily while wearing it.

Melli reached her hand from her bed, touched his cheek and said to him, "It is very nice out you go and play." She smiled at him but in her mind she was thinking about something else. She thought, "If the princess goes out with her son, I will go into the room and see what she's hidden in that bag. If she has any gold in there, then I will know for sure that she is the princess."

The princess knelt at her feet and said, "Yes, Melli has a good idea. We will go together. Give me your hand."

As soon as they were outside, Melli rose to her feet. She waited until they went farther away and then she went to the next room. She moved quickly to the floor and looked under the bed. She saw only a flower and the empty bag on the floor between the bed and the wall. That was not what she was looking for. "Why," she said. "Why is she hiding this? I'm surprised she ran and fell into the water for this flower!" She rose up and looked around the room but could see nothing else. Quickly she left the room, closing the door, before the princess came back and sat near the chimney. She was very confused. Is she the princess or someone else but she still did not understand why she was keeping that flower a secret from her. It seemed strange to her and she remained confused.

The next morning when the princess woke up she looked at her son. He was having trouble moving his arms and legs, and was missing his usual smile.

The princess picked him up from the bed and held him in her arms. She touched his forehead and he was burning up. She didn't know what was wrong with him until she went to the other room and saw Melli still lying on her bed. Right away the princess knew that something was happening. She went close to Melli. Slowly she removed Melli's hand, from her face but it was strange. Melli's skin had started to change and her eyes looked red. She was horrible looking.

The princess immediately rushed to the next room in the direction of the flower but it was too late. The flower had already started to change. Leaves were beginning to fall. She picked it up and rushed to the door. She thought at first that Melli could see the flower. With a demanding voice she said to Melli, "Tell me the truth, did you go in the room? Did you see anything in there?"

Melli barely talked to her, "Yes. I did. I just wanted to know what you were keeping hidden from me at all times."

As the princess was listening to her something came to her mind. She did not say anything to Melli. She put her son on the bed next to Melli and then she ran into the next room. She put the flower in the bag and tied a brown kerchief around her head. Quickly she came out of the room and went to the chimney. She reached her hand to one side and dug for some soot to blacken her face so that she would not be recognized.

She had in mind to go to the market but did not know the way. A second later she turned and moved closer to Melli. She asked her, "Tell me the way to get to the market."

"Why do you want to go this time?" Melli asked.

"I have a gift but it belongs to God and he may take it from me if he chooses. Just as he gave it to me, so I have to pass it on to someone else, and save my son," said the princess as her voice stopped.

Melli could not breathe and could barely move her lips to say anything. She took a minute to answer her. "Go in the direction of those tall oaks at the west of the forest. After you pass those then walk a long sloping hill. Don't worry about anything but keep going up until you see a village and then you will see the market."

The princess wanted to promise her that she would save her, but Melli looked very ill. "Hold my son's hand. There isn't much time," said the princess as she stepped out of the house.

Melli remained at home with her body shaking. She had an unexplainable sickness. The pain was getting worse and worse, but she still tried to talk to little Sandri. "Don't worry little boy, your mother will soon be back."

Little Sandri could not move at all and his breathing was very slow. He seemed to be near death.

The princess had passed the big, tall oaks and reached the village in half an hour. She was afraid and so terrified. She thought that even with her dirty face someone might recognize her. She was in an area that she'd never been before and didn't recognize anything in the village. The street was very narrow and crowded with people walking like crazy everywhere. It was something different for her to see and everything felt very strange. As she waked farther she stopped in front of an old house. She waited and waited but no one stopped near to even look at her. A few yards away from her were some elderly people sitting on little wooden stools by the door with several children playing outside their homes. As the princess was watching them she could hear their screams of joy and it made her feel sad that her child would never be able to do that.

After a while she started walking slowly. There was not really room for her to pass side by side of the people. They scrambled and pushed her to get out of the way but no one would think that she could be the princess because her face was so blemished. She looked like a poor and dirty woman.

Then a young woman came close to her. The princess rushed in front of her, shivering all over her body, and said to her, "Would you like a flower?"

The woman looked at her and said, "Yes, I would like one. Let me see it first."

Immediately a smile spread across the princess's face. She thought that the woman was going to take her flower. Quickly she opened the bag. In that moment her face changed when she looked inside. All the leaves of the flower had fallen down into the bag, and there remained only the stick set in the cup. Slowly she pulled it out and showed it to her.

When the woman saw it, she just walked away and did not say anything. But the princess ran after her, grabbed her arm, and said, "Take it please, it will bloom again."

The woman stopped and said, "Are you trying to fool me? I don't have time for this," and pushed her way.

"Take it please, it will make you happy later," said the princess as she begged her with all her soul.

The woman gave her a weird look but didn't say anything more and just walked away.

A few hours passed and the princess could not pass the flower on. She begged people to take it but some of them did not even stop and some, when they saw just a stick set in a cup, simply walked way.

The princess was barely walking. She was getting very tired, and couldn't think of what to do. Her arms and legs felt numb, her eyes swollen and red from the tears that she cried. Nothing was left for her to do but to walk back to her son with her shriveled flower that she could not give to anyone.

After she arrived near the tall oaks, she stopped and leaned back on a tree for several minutes, crying with tears like rain. She lifted herself off the tree and dropped on her knees. She opened the bag for the last time and looked inside it. She started talking to the flower, "I don't know if I will find my son alive. I kept you safe up until now. I know you must go but please leave my son with me. He is the only one that gives me hope in my life." As she was still talking, a few yards away from her, something was moving behind the bushes. Very quickly she turned her head and looked around but did not see anything. Slowly she closed the bag and put it close to the tree. She stood up and began to run to the house where her son was lying.

After she left, the bushes start moving again. Slowly out came Lanti with a small lamb tied to a rope held in his hand. He saw a woman walking away from the market carrying the same bag that his mother had before. So he followed her until she left the bag in the forest.

He got close to the bag, and slowly he opened it. He looked inside and he was surprised by what he saw. He knew what it meant because his mother had told him everything about the flower inside the bag. Quickly he closed the bag and took it with him as he turned to go back to the village.

In that moment at the old house in the forest, a zephyr of chimes passed through the room, blowing on Melli's face and little Sandri's body. Suddenly little Sandri started moving his fingers and Melli opened her eyes.

By the time the princess reached the house she had no more energy, even to open the door. She was afraid at that moment. She thought she might have run out of time and wouldn't see her son alive. With a trembling hand she pushed the door and walked in. As soon as she saw them in front of her eyes she started screaming loudly with joy and ran to hug them. She was filled with joy when she saw her son alive once again. She picked him up and hugged him with all her heart.

Melli turned her back, slowly walked to her bed and before she sat, she said, "I am so glad you are back to see for yourself that the little boy is all right." Then she sat on her bed and said, "I hope you will forgive me for what I did."

The princess looked at her and said, "Forgive you for what?"

"When you went outside I peeked into your room because when I was at the market I heard the princess was lost with a little boy and I thought if you had any gold in that bag that you kept hidden I would know that you were the Princess," said Melli.

The princess went near her and said, "I will tell you something but you have to promise me that you won't tell anyone."

Melli said, "Don't say anything. I know who you are. After I lost my sight, even when I thought that I would never see again, and you brought it back to me, I promised that I would not let you feel the pain again. You will stay with me, and we will live together here."

"I can't. I just need you to tell me where I can go," said the princess.

"No, you cannot go yet," said Melli. "You have to stay until you discover where to go and how to live."

"Yes, you are right, I have to learn everything in the villages," said the princess.

She thought it was going to be a beautiful beginning until she decided to go to the market early one morning a week later. She took some wool and put it in a big bag. She went near Melli, who was still in bed, and said, "We should go to the market today. Can we?"

"I don't want your son to go there, but you can go," said Melli as she looked at her, "With that dirty face, I don't think anybody would recognize you."

The princess still had a fear, but she had to go, and help Melli to live, so she left her son at home with Melli until she returned.

On the way to the market she stopped near the tall oaks. She looked by the tree where she had left the bag but she did not see it. She thought that someone could have found it and picked it up. So on one hand she was happy and on the other she was concerned because whoever took the bag would not understand what was inside it.

Once she had reached the market the people had begun their work as usual. She walked slowly on the dusty road carrying the bag of wool over her shoulder looking for a corner to stop and stay until she sold it.

She went to a corner behind an old house and stayed. She waited several minutes but no one came near her. After a short time a few yards away from her something was moving under some old sacks.

She turned her head once then looked back. She thought it was just a wild cat but when she looked back again she saw a young boy that awakened by digging in his ear with his finger and shaking his head to get the hair out of his face and put his hat on. It was Lanti with his small lamb next to him.

Are you ill? Have you been sleeping here all night?" the princess asked.

"Yes." he said, as he straightened up and rubbed his eyes. He knelt down again next to the old sacks that he was covered with all night and placed them one by one in the corner. He looked at the princess and smiled saying, "I need these again for tonight."

The princess froze for a moment when she saw what was beside him! Then her whole body began to tremble. It was the same bag that she had left by the tree a week before.

Lanti didn't know who she was and that was good because if had known he might have screamed in the market to tell everybody that she was the princess as he did for Sandri. But he saw she looked worried about something and moved closer to her. He put his hand on her arm said, "Are you selling this stuff or do you need any help selling what you have?"

Slowly, and with some reluctance, she said, "Yes, if you could."

"Yes." Lanti said slowly, "But when I help somebody they give me something to eat." The princess agreed that whatever he sold she would to give him half of it. He looked around at the street and said, "I think we can do this."

He did not just sit down and wait for someone to come to him like the princess did, but he got down on his knees and started to beg the people to buy the wool. He knew how to sell it. He took out half of the wool and showed it to the people who passed close to him and asked if they wanted to buy it. It took him about a minute to sell the wool.

The princess was surprised and said to herself, "I know why his clothes are so gritty and dusty. He works too hard."

After he finished his job he returned to the princess. He gave her one coin and kept the other for himself. "You may go home now," said Lanti, and he turned to leave. He had only gotten two steps away from her before she stopped him to ask, "Where do you live?"

He answered, "I don't have a home, I'm hungry and I have nothing to eat, so I'm going."

He left but the princess could not go back home and leave the bag with him without telling him what was inside of it. She didn't know that he already knew about the flower. So she went after him, caught up with him and said firmly, "Do you want to come to my house? You can eat there."

He seemed to have no worry for anything as he rushed toward her. He did not wait to be asked twice.

Before they left, he said to her, "Can you help me a little. Which you want to hold? This bag or this rope. Pick one."

She could not take the bag in her hands again. She seized the rope with both hands as quickly as she could and said, "Yes, I will take the lamb."

They begin walking. She could not say anything to him yet. She just walked after him with the weariness which was back in her heart again.

He initially thought that she had her home somewhere close to the market. When he saw that she was heading in the direction of the forest, he stopped, stayed where he was, and asked her, "Where is your house?"

"You need to pass through this forest and there is my house, not too far away," she said.

He took several quick steps back when he heard her. He did not want to go with her. He wanted to turn back.

At that moment the princess started shaking from the fear that maybe he would not come with her. She got close to him, started begging him and with a soft voice said, "You'll come with me, because I'm afraid to go alone in that scary forest. So can you come with me now please?"

Lanti thought for a moment and then said, "Yes I will come with you, but I hope I will remember how to return."

When the princess heard him she looked at him with a smile on her face and said, "I am sure that you will remember how to come back. I see how intelligent a boy you are. If I were just a little bit like you I would dance for joy."

After a time they neared the house. Melli was looking through the window of her small room. She saw someone was coming. She did not know who they were because they were still far away. Her whole body began to tremble as she ran toward little Sandri. She took him in her arms and looked in the room for a place to hide him. From the fear she lost her mind and could not think where to go. With her feet shivering she ran to the next room. She put Sandri away from the door and she returned to support the door with all the power that she had to keep it closed.

Before the princess and Lanti entered the house, the princess stopped and said, "You wait out here until I come back out." Then she opened the door slowly. She did not see her son or Melli in the first room but she heard a noise coming from the next room so she went and knocked on the door.

Melli heard the knocking, but she was afraid to open the door. She thought it was someone else but when she heard the princess's voice she was released from her fear. She opened the door very slowly. Her face was pale from the fear. With a broken voice she said to the princess, "You scared me! I thought it was someone else."

"Yes, you are good. There is someone else but he is outside," said the princess.

Melli came out of the room saying, "You know if someone sees your son they will know immediately so you cannot let anyone inside the house."

The princess, as she walked away from Melli and moved her head slowly from side to side, said, "No, He couldn't know that. He is too young to understand anything."

Melli looked from the window to see him. Immediately she knew him. She wanted to tell her who he was but she remained silent. She walked across the room and start talking with her hands.

The princess looked at her as she moved close to her and grabbed her hand, "Stop! What's happening to you?" asked the princess.

"I know that boy," Melli said. "He stays all day at the market. He lives there on the street and he knows all the world news. Now, if he enters here, he will know right away who you are."

"Slow down. Don't worry. He won't know. You have become more worried than me," said the princess.

Melli, as she looked her straight in the eyes without blinking, asked her, "Why did you bring him here?"

With a smile the princess answered, "I promised him that he could eat here. Now he is waiting outside the door and wants to come in." Then she stopped and started to feel the same pain that that she had a week before. "He saved my son and also you. Last week, I begged all the people that I met at the market to take the flower but none of them accepted. I left it by a tree and he took it. And now I want to help him as if he was my son." At that moment, while the princess was still talking, Lanti opened the door and slowly stuck in his head. With a soft smile he said, "I think you forgot me outside."

When Melli saw him at the door and that he already entered she said, "You can come in, the door is open now."

He came in slowly, and stopped in the middle of the room with his mouth open. He was surprised to see all the meat was hanging from the ceiling. "I am very hungry," he said.

Melli already had something cooking in the pot so she welcomed him to eat.

The princess could not eat anything. She was worried and concerned about how to begin to ask him to stay until he understood the flower. She could not let him go.

Then the door behind them burst open. Little Sandri came from the next room. He started walking very slowly toward his mother. He hugged her by hiding his face in her side.

"Don't be shy my son. This other boy is just a friend," the princess said to him while rubbing his back.

Slowly little Sandri raised his head and looked at Lanti.

"Boo!" said Lanti to make him scared but little Sandri just laughed and kept hiding his face in his mother side.

After a short time Lanti finished eating. The princess took a few deep breaths and then turned to face him, saying, "I want to ask you something."

Lanti started laughing aloud. "What? Would you ask me to pay for the food?"

Melli had left the room because she simply could not listen to how she explained the flower to him.

The princess lowered her voice and said to him, "You can stay here and work a few years until you grow a little and you can build your own home."

Lanti stood up and raised his voice, and said, "No! I cannot stay here. No way." He thought that she would force him to stay so immediately he ran toward the door and went outside.

Melli heard that he had run from the house so she came out of the room and said to the princess, "I already told you, you need to tell him and let him go."

The princess was worried, she thought that he would leave the flower with her again and things would become even worse than they were. With a sad look she said, "It's not just to tell him, but to help him."

"Are you mad at him?" asked Melli.

"No, no I'm not mad at him. It wasn't his fault," said the princess. She felt awful that she could not give any advice to him about the flower. Slowly she went outside to talk with him again. Maybe he would change his mind.

Lanti was at the cattle shed in the middle of the sheep looking for his lamb that he left before he came into the house.

The princess approached him and said, "I asked you whether you would like to stay here or let me help you."

He moved to the right by the tree and looked her square in her eyes for a moment and then looked down.

Her heart pounded as he lowered his head, she thought it would be difficult for her to make him stay.

She lowered her head near to his right ear and whispered, "You don't have to think about it, you just have to say yes. I'm staying," as she raised her voice a little bit higher.

"What do you want with me?" he asked her.

"I know that you want to go but I want to help you," she said.

He kept darting his eyes around and removed his hat. He started chewing on it. He had a very bad habit. Always when he got excited he put the tip of his hat in his mouth and chewed it like gum. "I cannot believe you really want me around forever," he said.

"Yes," she said. "I want you to stay here. See, your lamb also loves to stay here. Do you like that?" She tried to make him laugh.

"Oh, no," he said, "the lamb is not mine. I am just keeping it until my friend returns from the castle." He pointed his finger at the princess like he knew something. "Four soldiers from the kingdom beat him up for no reason. I didn't understand why they took him, because I know that person very well, he is extremely kind."

The princess couldn't say anything. She was in awe.

Lanti began to laugh a little and said, "I want to stay but I do not understand you either. Why do you want to help me? All the people at the market know that I live on the street, but none of them attempt to help me." And he turned his head away from her.

The princess addressed him with soft words, "You're not the only one without a home. I want to help because someone helped me before and I know how you feel when someone helps you."

Melli was looking from inside the house. She did not know what was happening with them but hoped for the best. She said in her mind, "How is she going to stay at home if she keeps him here, always with a dirty face, I cannot believe that she wants to do this."

An hour had passed by the time Lanti finally decided to stay. He was happy to have someone to care for him but he could not stay on without going back to the market.

He promised the princess that he would not stay long at the market. He would come back again.

Darkness came and Lanti did not return from the market. The princess started getting worried and could not sleep at all. She just sat near the window and kept waiting to see if Lanti would show up again.

Melli was lying in her bed. She could not sleep when she saw the princess waiting near the window. Looking at her she said, "I guess you were thinking of him. I think you worried a little too early."

"Yes. Well, I do not know," said the princess as she turned and went to sit in the next room full of sad thoughts. That night she lay awake thinking of Lanti and looking at the bag that she had in the room again.

The morning came and Lanti still did not return. The princess was very worried and could not think of anything else besides going to the market to look for him.

Melli was still lying on her bed when the princess came out of her room. She raised her head and looked at her. "It's only been a night. Do you want to go and look for him at the market?" Melli asked.

The princess didn't respond.

Melli spoke again, "I know that you are worried about him so you can go and look for him. I know that you will find him in the same place where you met yesterday but just beware when you go."

"Yes. I am going," said the princess, "If I am late please take care of my son."

Melli wrinkled her face and said, "Don't be worried about your son. Pretend he is with you. So go and don't be late."

The princess left for the market in hope that she would meet with Lanti again. She was not afraid anymore to walk on the road. She learned a lot of things in just a week about standing in the middle of people and facing them.

When she reached the market she was surprised. The road was clear. Just some elderly people sitting by the corner of some old houses. She knew that she would not find him there.

# CHAPTER 10

The queen had not yet lost hope even though it had been a week since she had seen her daughter. She still thought that someday her daughter would return home.

Drof was walking through the corridor in the direction of the imperial room. As soon as he opened the door he said to the queen, "You should come out now. Are you ready?"

The Queen was near a table. She had turned her back and was covering something with a cover, and put it in a small bag. She did not say anything to Drof. She just held her head down for a few seconds and took a deep breath. She turned to walk out the door with the bag in her hands.

She walked through the corridor with Drof following her. He wanted to know what she was holding in her hands, so very slowly he asked her. "What do you have in that bag my queen?"

She stopped for a moment and said, "Do you have ready everything that I asked for?"

"Yes, my queen," he said and turned his head the other way.

When they reached the end of the corridor, Drof ran before her. The queen entered the castle yard and Drof opened the fortress doors.

Outside the castle yard was full of people. They were staring at the queen, whispering among themselves, but they still did not know why they had been summoned. They just heard the bell and all had come to see why the queen had called.

The queen slowly went to her place and sat in her chair and put down the bag that she had in her hands. With her hand raised, she called Drof nearby, "Go and bring him here."

"Yes, my queen," said Drof as he moved toward the doors to enter the castle.

The queen looked worried. It was difficult for her to decide what to do, but she already had made up her mind.

A few minutes later, Drof came out with Sandri by pushing him by his arm. He pushed him in front of the queen and he turned to her saying, "I just need you to tell me what to do with him and I will do it." He acted very badly in front of her.

The queen shook her head and said brightly as she straightened up, "Get out of my sight, please."

Then Drof slowly moved away but he was not happy at all.

Sandri was kneeling beside the queen with his mouth open.

The queen began to walk around him saying, "Do you have anything to say before I speak?"

"No, my queen." he said as quietly as possible.

The queen took her position in front of the people. She began to speak in a voice of great pleasure. "I called you here because I want to tell you of a man who broke several laws. He did not truthfully answer some questions that I asked him."

Sandri did not want to answer the truth because, first, he did not know that the princess had a child, second, he did not have the courage to say anything to the queen.

Everybody began to speak with each other asking, "What did he do that we have not heard about?" "No one knows anything about him," a woman said.

The queen turned to sit. She did not want to speak anymore, because she thought that Sandri would faint with fear.

After the queen sat, the voice of a young boy came from among the people. It was Lanti leaping over a low stone, trying to see the queen. He yelled with a loud voice, "Why do you punish that man. He is not guilty, believe me my queen." He was still speaking when someone grabbed his arm to stop him from speaking. When he turned to see who was grabbing him he screamed even more. It was the princess trying to stop him but he did not listen to her. He was pushing her and trying to get away from her. By accident he grabbed her dress and ripped it in front of her neck and out came her necklace that she had never removed since her father had given it to her.

The queen was surprised. She stood up with eyes wide open and she tried to see as an owl in broad daylight. She took some steps forward. "Please stop," she yelled. She looked once with attention then turned back and sat on her chair. She lost her train of thought for a moment. She did not believe what had just shone into her eyes. It was the same ray she saw from the window, coming from her daughter neck just before the king's death. She had never forgotten it.

She was saying in her mind, "Is it my daughter? Do I really see her with my eyes?"

She sat in her chair for a minute and looked down at the people, but she quickly got up and whispered to Drof saying, "Go shut the doors of the fortress quickly."

Drof did not understand why she wanted to close the doors but he knew she was doing something she did not want to explain to him.

He did not go. He did not want to depart from the queen. He tried to hear everything that she was saying so he sent a soldier to close the doors.

The princess had no idea that her mother had seen her, but she looked around furtively to see if anyone was staring at her.

She began to walk slowly, directly toward the doors. By the time she reached the doors, the soldier already had closed them. When she saw the doors were closed she began to worry more.

The queen started talking. "I did not call you here only for the punishment of this man, but also for something that will make everyone happy." "Today would be the day," then she stopped talking. She went near her chair and slowly fell to her knees. She picked up the bag and opened it. Slowly she stood up and turned from the citizens. She took out something that caused all the citizens to remain frozen for a moment with mouths half open, staring at the queen.

The queen raised it high with her hands and said, "This is the crown of the king. Today I will put it on someone who is faithful and intelligent."

Drof was standing near her chair. He started to smile a little, because he thought that he was the only faithful man.

However, the queen took a step toward Sandri and put the crown on his head. She grabbed him by his arm, helped him stand and looked into his eyes, "Do you know who you are now?"

He was still afraid and his feet trembled. With a lower voice, he said, "With my understanding, the king."

"Yes. From now on you are the king," said the queen, smiling at him. "It was my hope that you would bring my daughter back."

Everyone was delighted to see the new king, but the princess didn't look up to see who had become the king.

She was too busy trying to find a way to get out of there. She could not wait until her mother finished her speech and had the fortress doors opened, but the queen did not finish yet. She started walking slowly down the stairs then rushed forward toward the people. All of them stopped whispering and looked at her in surprise, wondering where she was going. They cleared a path, one by one, until she arrived to face the poor woman.

People were staring at the princess. All they could see was a poor woman with a dirty face looking very frightened in front of the queen, but they still did not know who she was.

The princess turned her head finally to meet her mother but could not say anything. She stayed in place shaking from the fear caused by her mother looking at her for almost a minute without speaking. The queen was so glad to see her but still could not believe she was seeing her daughter's face again.

She tapped her daughter on the shoulder and asked with a soft voice, "Are you happy to see me again? It is pleasant to see you my daughter in good health," but the queen did not want her to answer, she wanted to see her up there nearby Sandri so that she could continue her speech, "Come with me now."

The princess's tears were streaming down her face and she couldn't stand it anymore. She began to walk after her mother up the stairs with her head down. Sometimes when she looked at her mother as they were walking up the stairs she wondered if her mother hated her so much that she might kill her any moment.

Lanti passed through the crowd. He thought the queen took her because of him, for telling him to stop when he yelled for Sandri. He turned toward the people and proudly said, "You see, I saved one and made another worse again. Now I must go and save her too." He continued to go toward the stairs.

The people began to laugh at him and could not believe that he would really go after the queen.

When the queen and the princess topped the stairs, the princess raised her head and stopped immediately in front of Sandri with her feet trembling. She was surprised when she saw that he was the one to become king. It was the man that she had never forgotten.

Sandri began to smile at her, raised his hand to take hers and escort her to the queen's chair. The princess's face was still dirty and she had a scarf over her head. It would have been difficult for most to recognize her, but not for Sandri. He had never forgotten her either.

The queen turned toward the people and said, "You all know that my daughter was lost and we could not find her. She has now been found!" and she pointed toward princess Artella.

Just as Lanti neared the queen he heard her speak those words. The woman that wanted to help him was the princess. With eyes wide open he stopped where he was and took his hat off right away. He put the tip of the hat in his mouth and started chewing it.

The princess was an unforgettable woman. Everyone remembered that she had acted crazy for a while. Nobody had recognized her until the queen pointed her out. The queen slowly approached her and said, "I found all of your secrets after you left. Now you should say something to the people, but do not say anything about the secret rooms."

The princess took two steps forward as she looked at her mother, surprised. She stood before the crowd and took a deep sobbing breath. "It was a strange step for me to go out of the castle where I had never been before but I learned so many things," said the princess as she turned her head and looked at her mother once. "I know all of you thought that I was a sick person. Yes, the pain and secrets that I carried made me sick in my mind. I know my mother will punish me, but for my son, if you please, leave him with his father who is now the king."

Sandri watched her silently. He could hardly believe that she was the mother of his child.

The queen approached the princess again with tears in her eyes and said, "If you want, you can stop now."

"No, mother, I want all to hear the truth." She returned and continued speaking. "The mistake that occurred I could not share with anyone, even my mother, because I felt ashamed. After my son was born, I felt no more shame, only pride," and then she stopped. She could not talk anymore. She walked back, wiping her face.

Sandri approached her and began to dab her face, wiped off the tears and kissed her on the forehead.

Freedom for her came from telling the truth and that emptied her chest of the sadness she had borne for two years.

Later that day, the princess took Sandri and the queen to Melli's house to meet her son. When they arrived, the princess said to the queen and Sandri, "Please let me let go into the house first so Melli will not become scared and run with my son."

Melli heard horses and looked out the window and was terrified. She ran over to little Sandri so she could try to hide him from the soldiers. As she stood looking from corner to corner the door swung open. It was the princess, who was hard for Melli to recognize because she was clean and dressed up. She looked very beautiful.

"It is ok Melli, it's me, Tella. Don't be afraid, everything is fine. The queen knows everything and I brought her and my son's father to meet you and my son."

Melli fell to her knees with relief and cried for joy. The princess rushed in and fell to her knees also and held Melli and her son in her arms and they all cried together with joy. When Sandri came in the door they all looked up and the princess smiled and said, "This is your son, little Sandri."

Sandri stepped forward, got down one knee and with tears on his cheek said, "You gave him my name," and he leaned forward and hugged them all.

After a moment the queen came into the room. Then little Sandri looked up and smiled at her and ran to her. He remembered her very well.

The queen smiled and reached her arms out to him, picking him up and holding him in her arms. She looked at Sandri and said, "Have you meet your son?" Sandri smiled and came to her and little Sandri held his arms out to his daddy. With great pride Sandri took him into his arms and turned to Artella and hugged her too.

Sandri and princess Artella were married and their son, little Sandri, stood with them.

Artella never wished she could have taken back that night that she slept with Sandri.

Sandri had been lucky to meet Artella. Something he would have never dreamt of.

The queen lived happily with her grandson that she loved so much.

After hearing that Melli and Lanti had helped her daughter she invited them to live in the castle forever.

Six years passed. Lanti met a girl and in his room something had started to happen. A new leaf just started to sprout on the flower that he kept in a bag.